I0684787

THE RUB

JA CARTER-WINWARD

BINARY PRESS 2012

Published By Binary Press Publications, LLC
ISBN-13: 978-1611710151
ISBN-10: 1611710154

Also By JA Carter-Winward

Falling Back To Earth
TDTM (Talk Dirty To Me)
Always Listen to the Ravings of a Mad Woman
(as JulieAnn Henneman)

～

Because of its tremendous solemnity,
death is the light in which great passions,
both good and bad, become transparent,
no longer limited by outward appearances.
~Søren Kierkegaard

PART I

September, 2010

1

Today had an augur of good fortune.

He had, after all, said *yes* to lunch. What else could he have said? It was about his wife. Chelle and Cliff smile at each other perfunctorily over their menus.

Chelle shifts her foot and topples her purse. The condoms inside scatter across the floor as if skidding across ice. She leaves her purse on its side. No one stops to pick the condoms up, including her.

Across the table, Cliff's eyes shift to the floor, the slick wood shiny and reflective. He stares at the spilled contents and finally tears his eyes away, careful and questioning.

"The Cobb salad is good, I hear." Cliff holds her eyes and she feels naked. Erect nipples prominently stand out from chilled breasts, like the condoms spinning across the floor in figure eights, they draw his gaze.

She studies her water glass. She can't speak and watches the condensation on the glass. Beads of water drizzle alone, then merge.

Small talk will normalize it. She can't speak.

Cliff clears his throat.

"I love Cobb salad," he says.

"I don't like egg in salad."

She regrets not liking egg in salad, now. Cliff's brow furrows. He studies the menu, seeking another selection for her. She didn't mean to shut him down but she wants to tell the truth. She will do this with integrity.

Her napkin slips to the floor and she blesses her luck. She pulls the condoms close to her, covers them with her shoe. The crackle of wrappers gets drowned out by the rumble of patrons in the hotel cafe. A draft throughout the café causes the plants to wave behind Cliff like fans. He looks like he could use a good fanning.

Sweat drips between her breasts even though the room is chilly. "You're probably wondering why I called—to meet you, I mean," she says.

"Well, yes and no. I was wondering how you've been," Cliff says. "I wondered if you looked the same."

She wonders if Cliff's wife looks the same. *Cunt. Whore.*

"Well, I'm right here." She mirrors him, hands resting politely on the table when she doesn't feel polite. She doesn't want to act cold or be cold. She's so tired of cold.

"Yes, yes, you are here. You look great, by the way."

"So do you."

"Eh, I'm still an average Joe." He laughs, looks around, and scrapes his chair as he scoots in closer.

She knows he says it to excuse Marilyn. Both men love her. *Cunt. Whore.*

"No, you're not average. You do look great. Not a day older." Like a painting; a suit. Like a room arranged perfectly, pillows just so. Organized disarray.

He doesn't deserve what she's doing to him.

"Well, it's been what, four years? At our age, things slide south faster every day."

"Yeah. Four years. God…it's weird how time flies."

Across the aisle in the chapel, Cliff and his wife Marilyn sit with straight backs. They don't look at Chelle. She can't believe they came to the funeral. Their daughter didn't join them.

She forces the church interior from her mind by picturing him shirtless, on top of her, and warms when his brown eyes blink too rapidly. He's human, too. Like her.

"I've always thought you were very attractive."

"Thank you. I needed to hear that," she says, looking down at the menu.

"Yeah, it does a number on your ego, doesn't it?"

"It does. Yes. So, does Marilyn know you're here?"

"She doesn't ask. She doesn't have the right to ask."

Marilyn. *She* is Marilyn.

Cliff revoked his wife's rights. Chelle can see his backbone through his chest now and it makes him taller.

"So, how are you?" Chelle asks. The outside world intrudes in the form of bus boys filling their water glasses. The room is white except the plants and the floor.

He has sad eyes now and all of her nervous energy throbs in her neck, creeps up her throat. She doesn't want to show him her wounds. If she does that, he'll understand why her husband strayed. Cliff will see her cold manner, her sagging breasts, her screeching vibrato when she tries not to cry.

"I'm doing just fine. You?"

"I want you to fuck me." She lets her shoulders drop as she releases the thought that has curled in her mind for weeks. She could fall asleep right now, her head is so heavy. Had she slept a full night in four years?

He doesn't answer her, but there has to be a way to patch the hole in the ice.

ᔕ

Cliff felt badly about the small thrill he'd gotten from taking Chelle's call.

Marilyn hadn't asked who it was and that part stung a little; like jealousy would be the final and only proof that she wants him. Marilyn wouldn't leave; not physically. He was sure of that. The glue that binds them is sickly sweet, but not made for consumption. Its cloying scent underlies everything Marilyn and he do—even this meeting with Chelle in a hotel café.

The restaurant's clamor is comforting, as if the noise fills the spaces in between their words and takes the edge off. But the damn plants. The palms in back of him constantly brush his hair, as if God taps him. Reminds him.

And how badly he wants to tell Chelle's husband, Dan, that he isn't, hasn't been, won't be, the only one. That is Marilyn. It always has been.

Chelle, though, she's a loose cannon. She's a fiery woman who speaks plain and says her peace, and doesn't play too nice or too fair. Marilyn plays nice, but not fair. Never fair.

Chelle had arrived later than him and he suspects that was calculated. But then, he's been married to Marilyn for a long time.

They both hold Dan and Marilyn's love affair in front of their eyes like blinds, devices to open and shut at their leisure. When Chelle broached the subject, Cliff was relieved. He'd almost laughed; she'd taken the words right out of his mouth and he's glad. The words tasted bitter.

He'd gotten semi-stiff when the condoms fell out. Did she bring them for him? He could almost feel his fingers sink into her meaty body. Chelle's arms look so soft, pleasant, round and dimpled. So different from his wife. Chelle is Mother Earth and Marilyn, she's dry for him now, no longer fecund, no longer moist.

Marilyn's outside any sort of stereotypical woman. She can't be Mother Mary because she's like a whore. She can't be a whore because she's like Mother Mary. No, people want her because of a projected, inherent goodness that emanates from her. But the virtue hides another charm, another inherent purpose.

Marilyn has a plan. Always.

And maybe that's not fair. Marilyn is a good wife, a good mother. Her volunteer work at The Center has been recognized in news articles and in their community. So why does her involvement humiliate him? Why won't he help?

He shifts his eyes to Chelle's mouth, full and soft. He can't help compare. He sees Marilyn's shadow superimposed on her and then Chelle drowns her out. Chelle is the type of woman who bucks and sweats and growls when she fucks and Marilyn is silent, composed, muted, as if performing for a disapproving crowd.

His hands sweat and the menu blurs and then she mentions them both—her husband and his wife, and his relief is replaced by the desire to retreat to familiarity and safety. He suddenly wants to be home with

Marilyn and Callie, just them, their little family. *We are a family unit.* He doesn't know why that phrase comforts him, but it does.

And yet. Marilyn's arms keep appearing as tactile sensations under his fingers. He shudders at the thought of them. They are sticks with sinewy muscle from her Pilates workouts. His gaze shifts to Chelle's arm and he wants to sink his teeth gently into her bicep.

Her eyes aren't hungry, though. They could be, if he fancies them to be, but he knows *hungry*, at least he thinks he does. They look more like frightened animal eyes, looking at him sideways and holding still. She would bolt, and that thought makes his semi-erection quiver and grow. He's powerful.

Cliff stares into Chelle's eyes, wanting her to cower. He isn't sure how much of it has to do with her fleshy arms and hips and thighs. Her thighs and what's in between and the sweat... and he hopes to God she doesn't shave a little landing strip on her pussy. He wants hair to kiss his mouth and cheeks and he's throbbing hard now.

His wife seduced Chelle's husband; his daughter is alive. He can't think of anything to say. *What could I possibly have to say to Chelle Shaw?*

Being this broken in front of her is obscene. He has no right because his daughter is in her college class right now earning an *A* and being vibrant and beautiful like her mother. He is insipid in this yearning state. The strange mother-fantasy he has of Chelle and her earthy musk curling into his nose and saturating his mouth disquiets and excites him.

He has no right and then he gives himself the right when he thinks of Dan on top of Marilyn. Marilyn might buck for Dan.

He would make Chelle buck and groan for him and she can forget Dan and Marilyn and her daughter and his daughter and just think of him. *Only him.*

The room sways a little when Chelle tells him what she wants. He breathes in staccato; he can't back out now. But he swears that he sees his neighbor from two doors down watching him through the palms.

He has to piss. The delicious hardness he'd felt at lunch subsides with each step to the hotel room. And he has to piss. As he walks he adjusts his waning hard-on. This only serves to expose him to his zipper through his fly opening. The zipper scrapes his dick and he winces. He doesn't look, but he hears Chelle's soft steps behind him.

Cliff enters the hotel room, excuses himself and ducks into the bathroom. The harsh light over the mirror makes the circles under his eyes seem smudged in, like he'd used a pencil, or like after football practice. He stares at his face and wonders what happened to his upper lip. He knows he had one at some point.

Cliff finishes and flushes but before he puts it away, he strokes it. His cock feels like it's been dipped in numbing solution.

Fuck. C'mon.

He sees lotion and opens it, then thinks again. What if Chelle wants to go down on him? She'd get a mouth full of...*honey-lime verbena lotion.* What if she's one of those women like Marilyn who has the cunt of a histrionic hypochondriac?

All of this hasn't helped his cock get any harder and so he pictures Chelle in the room, lying down spread eagle on the bed. He imagines her pussy open to him. Her olive-skinned legs are bent up and when he comes out, still dressed, he'll eat her. By then, he'd be hard enough.

He turns out the light and walks out but Chelle isn't where he hoped she'd be. He isn't stupid enough to think she'd be spread eagle, but maybe her fucking *purse* could be on the fucking *table*, at least.

Numb, numb, numb.

Her eyes widen as he approaches her and the lost look has been replaced by something he hopes is lust; playful, with a touch of...what is it?

She looks like she could bite now. But he doesn't want it like this. He rolls his shoulders back and imagines his chest expanding with strength. Chelle is immobile, the look in her eyes disconcerting, and now he isn't sure what he wants.

He ought to say something. Like before you lower someone into the ground. *A few words.*

Before Cliff can speak, she does. And he listens to her talk about his wife and her husband. His jaw freezes and sets in taut alignment. In some distant place in him, Cliff has held the illusion that it's all been a dream. Chelle, in her mercy or madness, strips him of all of that and in just a few words, it becomes real.

∽

The hotel clerk doesn't look twice at Chelle. He only gives her apathy and she gets enough of that. She wants to tell him she ate at the café. She wants to tell him why she's there. She wants him to care.

Cliff leads the way to the elevator and he no longer seems tall. She wants to conjure the same quiver from lunch but it dissipates with the ascent of the lift.

Three, two, one. Take off.

The hall hums in a strange silent vibrato and her legs wobble, rubbery from the elevator ride. She runs her hand along the rough wall paper lining the hall, feigning indifference. She earned this and she already feels like a whore.

Cliff slides the card key in and out. Not too slow, not too fast. Perfect— like the space between his eyes. Symmetrical.

The gooseflesh on her arms stands at attention with the chilly room that's so dark. She hopes he keeps the lights off. Instead he turns them on, which illuminates the miniature hall dividing the bathroom from the bed. The light falls unattractively on Chelle's face in the full length mirror on the closet.

Cliff immediately steps into the bathroom. "Why don't you get comfortable?" he says as the door closes.

The bed spread is pristine and she sits. Her purse rests on her lap; she can't bring herself to place it on the table. She's glad no mirror stares back at her now. She's glad her bra and panties match.

Then it hits her—a sublime moment that borders on elation, like toppling a house of cards, or worse, a child's sky scraper made of wooden blocks. She doesn't know how she'll keep from saying it.

Cliff comes out of the bathroom, shirt outside his pants and she stands. She feels the words erupting out of her and she can't stop them—won't stop them.

"Do you know how I found out?"

"About...?"

"Dan. Your wife."

"No, I...no." Cliff recoils slightly because this may not be the road he wants to take. It suddenly occurs to Chelle that her road and his road may be light years apart and she feels like a whore again.

She can't read Cliff's expression. She doesn't know if she should continue. She knows all of Dan's expressions but Cliff's are foreign to her.

Dan and Marilyn. It sounds so much better than *Dan and Chelle.*

She wants to hurt Cliff, not just for his wife's sins, but for his daughter's, too. She approaches him slow and careful, ready to turn on the iciest cold shower he's ever had. But she wants her words to heat him before they douse him.

"Dan came home late one night and I'd been drinking with a girlfriend, you know?"

He nods his head in slow motion, eyes never leaving her face.

"She and I had kissed, and I was hot and ready for him, for Dan..."

She gets lost in that moment for a while, that pure moment when she thought she was the only woman in Dan's bed.

"Yeah, so he came home and I seduced him. I knelt in front of him and took his pants down, watching his eyes. He had a hard time staying on his feet because he was drunk."

I could smell her perfume even as I pulled his chinos down around his ankles and I did what wives do to create imaginings and paranoia—the stuff hot, passionate pain-sex is made of.

"I wrapped my mouth around his cock and I tasted her. He'd been in Marilyn just an hour before. Maybe less."

She wonders if she pushed too far. His eyes are ghostly; pale, colorless orbs regarding her, mustering heat that may never be there for her. She continues, voice soft.

"I took him deep in my mouth, down my throat, to that place where you gag, you know? And I tried to ignore the taste, that *taste*. But my spit made his dick wet again. When I wiped my mouth, I knew. It wasn't me. Couldn't have been me."

Cliff's voice rasps half alive from him. "Why are you telling me this?"

"So you know. So you know that it's real."

His mouth twitches for one, brief moment. Then his eyes close.

2 _____

Dan Shaw taps all four bobble-headed football players on his desk with a sharpened pencil. Dan mimics the toys with his own version of bobble-heading as his shift manager stands in the doorway, whining.

"Mr. Shaw, I'm frustrated because they aren't hustling like they should be and this is not the kind of work UPS—"

"Jerry," Dan smiles, "let me talk to them. You just go on break, relax, have a cup of coffee. Hell, go in the bathroom and jack off. Do what you wanna do. Okay? I've got this."

Jerry looks down and Dan reminds himself to touch base with him later. After he's calm. After he whacks off in the bathroom. Everyone knows he does it.

The door closes behind Jerry and Dan lets his gaze fall on the two men sitting in his office. They try—and fail, not to snicker. "Okay, okay, look. Jerry's right. You guys are old timers and you represent what we stand for here. And I'm not so much worried about the younger guys, and gal, that you work with."

They groan when he mentions the one woman who works on the dock.

Dan continues. "I'm worried ultimately about the customer and their packages. You guys fuck around, we make mistakes. Then know what happens? It looks bad for *me*. And it's all about how I look, understand?"

The two men nod. "Sorry, Dan. We was just playin'. You know us."

"Yeah, unfortunately I do. Look, think of it as you guys saving me from having to deal with Jerry every day, okay?"

Before they can laugh too loud, Dan interrupts. "Hey, now c'mon, Jerry's a good guy and we all know he's a hard worker. But he's a pain in my ass and he's near retirement, so let's just play nice until that day comes, hopefully by June. Okay? We a team?"

"Yeah, a team," says one.

"Whoohoo, go team," says the other.

"Alright, smart asses, quit fucking around and go to work. Remember, all about me. *Love me*, okay?"

They stand to leave and Dan pats their backs. "And don't walk outta here smiling. Look like I just kicked your asses, for God's sake."

Both men instantaneously wipe the grins from their faces and pseudo-grumble about Dan being a prick.

"A big prick, remember," Dan calls after them.

They laugh again and Dan holds up his finger to remind them.

He closes his office door and sits in his cushy swivel chair. He doesn't want to sit at the desk anymore. He wants to return to the old days when his back worked and he could toss boxes and heft the heavy loads with the young guys. When he'd hurt his back they put him on scanner duty. Then shift manager. Then he moved up with the appropriate combination of ass-kissing and smarmy-wise assed-ness that left his superiors wondering if he was serious, and the underlings snickering that he may not be.

He opens his game of Spider Solitaire and closes it again, deciding to work the dock today, just for kicks. He looks at the phone and closes out the game.

On his desk, the picture of his wife Chelle is a reminder to call, a reminder to feel, a reminder to hurt. If he visualizes photos of Marilyn on the desk before him, they appear in gilded frames. They make him want to clean off his desk and organize it. How much farther up would he have to go to deserve her? District Manager, maybe.

But she loves him now, small-timer that he is. Maybe she only seems to be into money. She doesn't seem to care when he's inside her, when she kisses his mouth and whispers to him that she's his. But sometimes when she says it, it sounds like she's placating a small child who's just brought home a macaroni necklace for his mother to wear to her party.

The swivel chair bangs on the bookcase behind him as Dan stands. He walks out of his office and heads for the dock, letting the door close behind him. He'll avoid the really heavy loads today, but he needs to throw something.

∞

Everything makes sense when the corners meet and match. The fitted sheets—now they are a different beast altogether. One has to create corners to fold them properly. And this is what Marilyn does.

Her favorite room is the laundry room because it's always warm and smells of Lavender Dreams fabric softener. She's made the room her own despite the bright fluorescent bulbs above. The lights rob the room of warmth.

Wooden plaques with words of inspiration hang haphazardly on the wall in front of her. As she folds, irons and changes loads she can see and remind herself to be grateful.

Gratitude, Dream, Love, Hope, Faith, Inspire, Believe.

Marilyn favorite is *Faith* because it's broken in half. She still sees the fissure where she'd hot-glued it together. Her daughter Callie had, in a fit of rage, pulled it from the wall and thrown it to the other side of the room. The wall it struck hadn't been marred, but the small sign had broken in two. For some reason, Marilyn held tenderness for the broken sign, as if it needed extra care and affection.

It didn't remind her of Callie. It only reminded her of the day that her daughter hurt something she loved. It was the first time Marilyn had seen it in Callie, her normally dulcet and compliant child. Over the years Callie's inner turmoil turned into outer dissent. The chaos bleeds out and over Callie and soaks into every encounter Marilyn and she have. Marilyn sighs. *Gratitude.*

The clock reads a quarter to three and she almost decides to leave the laundry to run to the bank. But an old familiar pull keeps her rooted to the spot. Callie would be walking in any minute.

She steels herself for the inevitable barrage of eye rolls, insults, and passive-aggressive comments from her daughter. She'd hoped that, at 19, Callie would be softer. But she has become more aggressive. They were talking about her moving out for her sophomore year.

Marilyn hears the car door slam and sees Callie approach through the window in the laundry room door. When Callie walks in, she seems monumentally irritated that Marilyn is in the room.

"It's like you wait here for me every day."

"I waited for you here every day when you were little, too."

"How 'bout you wait in the kitchen next time and make me a sandwich?" Callie smiles a saccharine smile and Marilyn laughs.

"I think you're a big girl and you can make your own sandwich."

"Yeah, God forbid you should make food."

"Hey, I make food."

Callie barks out a laugh as she leaves the room. "M'kay."

Marilyn wants to follow her, defend herself. How can she ignore the years and years she'd fed her? And, yes, now that she's in college, she doesn't cook as much, but Cliff's home later and later each night, and Callie won't eat most of what she makes.

Marilyn argues with Callie in her head until she satisfactorily shuts her daughter up.

The clothes are still warm from the dryer, but instead of completing the folding, she closes the dryer door.

She walks into the kitchen and pulls out bread and lunch meat. Callie likes turkey on sourdough.

൮

The Youth Suicide Prevention Center, or The Center, staffs three full-time office employees, one on-call doctor loaned out from St. Rose, two part-timers, and four crisis workers. Volunteers log in their hours weekly, with some people putting in up to 16 hours a week.

Many of the volunteers at YSPC are survivors of loved ones who committed suicide. Their particular brand of intervention is a wake-up call to those seeking to end their lives.

Many of the youth are in such pain, it's difficult for them to see the impact their actions would have on loved ones. As is true with many crisis centers, most of those who seek out services at YSPC are looking for a reason to live.

Monday afternoons are innocuous; deceitfully peaceful until shattered by the unexpected. Dan knows this and that is why he's here.

He gives himself double bonus points every time he walks through the door knowing Marilyn isn't there. She's the reason the place hasn't broken him to pieces already.

Of course, he'd started working there of his own accord a year and a half ago. He'd known Marilyn volunteered there, but he was not prepared for her brand of crisis intervention with him.

It's quiet with only a small pipe of music feeding over the speakers. Almost no one is there because it's noon, but he stays anyway, reading and sorting reports for a study being conducted at UNLV on teen suicide. He numbly peruses the notes and his heart both jumps and sinks at the sound of the front door bell.

A short Latino man has his arm protectively around his wife's quaking shoulders; they approach the desk with slow, measured steps.

"Buenos días. ¿Cómo puedo ayudarle—" Dan begins.

"I speak English." The man's face sweats profusely and his eyes dart to Dan and then around the front of the desk.

"Okay, what can we do for you?"

The man's lips move without speaking. He finally meets Dan's gaze. "We think...our daughter is planning to..."

The woman's howling cry pierces the silence and Dan comes around the desk and places his arm around her and the man. "Come back here, this way, okay? We can help, okay?"

Dan's pace is faster than theirs and his face is made of stone. They seem intent on shuffling and Dan wants to scream at them that they have no time—until they do. Until time is all they have.

They arrive at the back room where one of the crisis workers, Stacey, is sitting at her computer. She motions the couple inside the office.

He quells the need to ask them where their daughter is. *Who is she with? Does she have a plan? Is she safe?*

He quells it because it isn't his job, but his throat is thick with worry as the couple thanks him. The woman gazes at him for a moment.

"Gracias."

"No es nada."

Dan closes the door and leans against the wall. His breathing is labored. Sweat coats his upper lip. He squeezes his eyes shut for a moment, only to open them to the empty hall.

∽

She only regrets knick-knacks when she cleans.

Each one has to be moved and dusted, replaced, assessed; each one must go through the determination process. Has it been here long enough? Too long? What memory is attached to it, what does it portend?

It's a game Marilyn plays each week and it's the impetus for her shopping when she decides quickly and finally that something must be replaced. This week it's three Fleur de Lys sculptures that have graced her hallway table for too long. She moves them off of the table and sets them on the floor. She's transitioning from French Country to a more streamlined, simple décor. Minimalistic. *Simplify*. She decides she needs a new plaque on her laundry room wall.

It nags at her that Callie is on her computer all day after class and only works at the coffee shop two days a week. Marilyn's heart rate speeds up with the unspoken conflict arising within her. She argues with her daughter silently and knows she should be demanding more. But she can't. Callie holds her hostage.

She glances up the stairs and decides.

"Callie." She calls her name as she mounts the steps to the second floor. "Callie!"

"What?"

The computer flashes images and Callie minimizes the windows. Marilyn doesn't know whether she does research or watches videos.

"Are you busy?"

Callie raises her eyebrows and indicates the computer with her head.

"That isn't answering my question." Marilyn allows a half-smile to soften it.

"Yes, I'm busy. Sociology's a bitch." Her sullen face wards off Marilyn's advance into the room.

"Well, when you're done, I need some help with vacuuming."

"Why?" Callie's face is puzzled.

"Because the house needs vacuuming."

"Okay, and you can't do it because...?"

"Callie, you live here too. Dad works a hell of a lot more than you, and he helps clean."

"Yeah, well he's off when he's off. I'm never off. Know what I mean? *School* is constant. And you're not doing anything."

Marilyn bristles. The room is in organized disarray and she can't complain; she shouldn't complain. Nevertheless, the comment stings.

"I do a lot, Callie. I could use some help."

I'm the parent, goddamnit, and this is my house.

Callie looks back at her monitor and pulls up a website. She shuts Marilyn off, dismissing her with silence. Marilyn stares at her and wonders where she had gone wrong. Was she too easy on her? Did she give her too much?

"Callie. I'm asking for a little help, that's all."

"Why? Going to The Center again tonight?" Callie's look is derisive and Marilyn swallows thickly.

"No, I'm staying home and cooking a dinner for us. All of us."

"Whatever. I'm going out tonight, so don't make any for me."

"I was going to make your favorite—"

"Make dad's favorite, why don't you?"

"I—he eats whatever I make."

"Yeah, you could say that."

"What? What did you say?" Marilyn steps further into the room, her breath quickening, a warning glare in her eyes.

"I'm not going to be *home*, Mom."

Marilyn watches as her daughter minimizes a chat window that pops up.

Callie continues to peruse the site and Marilyn retreats silently from the room. Their words hang in the air like frost. Cliff won't talk to his daughter. He's held prisoner by her, too.

Back in the living room she replaces the Fleur de Lys on the table. The room is overwhelming now and the knick-knacks all seem to crowd around her like hungry mouths.

3

Callie places her pencil carefully by her paper. She still writes her assignments in longhand because she's in love with her cutesy girlish handwriting. All her letters are still round. Like a fucking child.

Back on her chat, she types in what she's wearing. What she's wearing is a large t-shirt and pajama pants. This is not what she types in her chat window. Her web cam is off, so she bullshits her way through everything until he wants to see something. And he always does. Callie's afraid he's losing interest. It had been a week. Today she'll give him a peek.

Callie likes pushing it. She hams it up, writing whatever he wants to hear. She's always good at saying what someone wants to hear. She can be whatever, whomever she wants to be. *A chameleon.*

She turns on her webcam, adjusts it, and peels off her t-shirt, touching herself, acting the slut for him. Then, as quickly as she starts, she pulls the large, blue shirt over her head again. The excitement lasts only seconds, and then it fades with the stillness on the screen. The words stop and the room is silent.

On the other end of the chat, Callie knows a middle aged man sweats and rubs himself off. He lives in Michigan. He never turns on his webcam. She wouldn't want to see him. He doesn't leave his small condo and he doesn't ever see the sun. He told her that to gain pity. All she can think of is how he must smell. He finally gets a look at her tits and she knows that's all he needs.

Callie doesn't know who "he" is, but he's old and he always asks her to wear boots. Maybe she'll find some at the mall now that fall is here, even though in Henderson it never gets cold enough for boots.

The monitor goes black as she puts it to sleep and stands, stretching her limbs and talking out loud. She talks only to herself, just to herself. She strokes herself better than all of the guys she lets in her pants.

Across the room, a drawer glows in the late afternoon. It glows with promises of calm, cool, warm—all at once. The drawer has a heartbeat.

She tries to tell herself that today she won't need one, but as she thinks it, she moves to the dresser. Inside the drawer, underneath her athletic socks, a baggy of yellow pills waits for her.

The yellow pills help Callie so she feels safe and in control. The yellow pills are a big fat fucking blanket, a cocoon in which she wraps her body and sleeps.

There are two pills in her hand and a half glass of watered down iced tea to wash them down.

In a few precious moments, she won't be angry at her mother. She won't be angry at her father. She almost decides to join them for dinner that evening but then she remembers her cocoon and how heavy it can be.

∽

Chelle's face stings from a strike that never came. She wants to be hit, to have something to rage against. But Cliff does the most inert thing he could do. He slumps onto the bed.

He won't meet her gaze, and so she pushes him gently by his shoulders onto his back. He allows her to push while his eyes stare, blank and shining, at the ceiling. She undoes his pants, reaching up to him with her eyes, but he stares straight up, breathing shallow and slow.

He's gone soft. She works him first with her hands, then her mouth, but she can't do that for long. He smells like Dan, like *man*, like every guy she'd sucked off since she first did it at twenty. She lays her cheek on his naked thigh and they are still.

∽

Chelle's mouth and hands are hot on his skin. Her long hair tickles his thighs. But Cliff's cock feels already spent and he wants to drift to sleep.

The pillow top mattress encases his body like a casket and his mind wanders to Chelle's daughter's casket and how Dan and Chelle held onto it before they closed the lid. Her name was Marin. Chelle had been heavier then, with tears watering her cheeks and shadows behind her eyes, as if a dark sheet had been pulled over her whole countenance.

Dan had openly sobbed. Their only child. Cliff felt their disillusionment, their guilt. It was everyone's fault.

Chelle's mouth is moving on his thigh. She's singing a soft song and he absently places his hand on her hair and brushes it away from her forehead.

She sings louder and he recognizes the song but not the group. The song's about flowers and soldiers and where had they all gone? He wants to ask her what she had sung to Marin because he can see she's the type of mother who would sing her child to sleep. But the subject is closed for him and she's singing a sad song already.

He sits up and Chelle shakes herself from her reverie of song. Cliff stares at her for a long time, wanting to ask her about surviving, wanting to ask about loss. All of it roils in his gut like interred lava, boiling, never to see the light of day.

Shiny eyes move back and forth on his face and he isn't sure how to mitigate his failure under Chelle's deft touch. He wants to tell her it has been a long day. He wants to tell her it isn't her fault, but it is. She carries silence with her that shouts much louder than clamoring bells. The lipstick is gone from her mouth, leaving her full lips rosy; her lips part. In her eyes, questions dance and twirl like chaotic nymphs and suddenly he sees all of her pain, or he imagines he does. He nods in acquiescence.

Chelle returns her mouth to him and he leans his head back as she pulls the ductile flesh of his limp cock into her mouth. He doesn't worry that he's soft. The delicious sensation of being soft in a woman's mouth is something he rarely, if ever, enjoys. And Chelle is languid and patient; the sight of her working him causes a twinge of heat, but then he sees her eyes and they are far away.

Cliff stops her and lifts her chin.

"Thank you," he says. He smiles and he can see she understands.

❦

On the stove, Hollandaise sauce bubbles in a slow, methodical boil and the aromas of chicken, ham, and Swiss permeate the house. Marilyn is making Callie's favorite.

Callie has been asleep in her room since four. It's seven now and Cliff isn't home. She knows better than to call the office. He's been off since noon. She knows better than to call his cell; she doesn't want to know exactly where he is or what he's doing. She just wants him home.

The chicken will bake for only 5 more minutes, then she will have to go wake Callie. Maybe Marilyn will ask her daughter to call Cliff.

Marilyn hears the garage door open and she jumps from her reverie to pull out the chilling salad.

Cliff walks in, hurried and out of breath. He puts down his bag and strides to her and she can't move but wants to back away from the feral look in his eyes. He grabs her by both shoulders and lifts, pulling her into him. His mouth collides with hers and all she can think about is the sauce and the chicken and how Callie is upstairs.

"Do you love me?" Cliff searches her face and she nods as he stares.

"Of course I love you."

It's all she needs to say to hear him breathe out in relief, but he doesn't let her shoulders go.

"You're hurting me, Cliff."

"Come to bed with me."

"Cliff…dinner—"

"Fuck dinner! Come to bed with me."

The timer beeps on the chicken and she turns and looks at the oven, then back at his searching gaze. He doesn't let her shoulders go, and she can't help but look at the oven once more.

Cliff releases her and she moves away quickly to retrieve the sizzling chicken. The slow boil of the Hollandaise had increased to large, purposeful bubbles, and soon, the creamy sauce is up and over the small pots' edge.

"Damn it!" Marilyn pulls the pan off of the stove.

Cliff clears his throat and his voice turns from husky to hollow. "Callie home?"

"She's sleeping. Will you turn the oven off? It's ready."

Cliff presses the "Off" button and watches his wife. She's aware of his stare. She can't go upstairs with him. Dinner's ready and Callie might wake.

"I'm going to get cleaned up and change."

"But Cliff, dinner's—"

"Keep it warm. It's not for me anyway."

He exits the room and Marilyn's stomach twinges. She's no longer hungry. She pulls her loose pants up to her hip-bones and stirs the boiling sauce one more time. The bubbles have stopped, but the sides and bottom are burned.

Marilyn hears Callie's music suddenly blast from her room. The noise is almost unbearable from the kitchen. Knowing Callie, she will be gone before Cliff is out of the shower. Marilyn puts a foil tent over the meat and mounts the stairs to their bedroom. She'll meet him in the shower.

4

The bottles remind her of Christmas. Maybe it's because Chelle's father lined up all of his liquor on the cabinet on Christmas Eve. Began drinking at noon. By three he was jovial and they basked in his child-like excitement while Mama clucked at him to stop dipping his fingers in the *arroz con leche*. By seven he beat Mama. By nine he was asleep.

The liquor bottles looked to Chelle like all the many ornaments on the tree. They hung there, alive, and filled with the promise of peace. She used to stand in front of it while Mama cried, and the lights would fade in and out of focus until Chelle just saw one giant glow.

She placed Limoncello and tequila in her cart, along with her red and white wines. She will splurge tonight and get a dessert wine—"ice wine", they call it. She'll drink ice wine and the sweltering heat will not consume her.

Chelle turns her cart and almost hits a young woman head-on. Their eyes meet. Chelle is still.

"Excuse me." Callie Erickson darts around her and walks quickly away. Chelle counts in her head. Had she forgotten how old Marin would be now? Eighteen? Nineteen? Nineteen. Chelle turns to see Callie grabbing a big bottle of tequila from off the shelf.

The checkout queues are sparse and Chelle heads for the front. Callie appears ahead of her, her long, dark-golden curls waving with her motion. Chelle stares at the back of Callie's head, mesmerized by the curly locks.

The girl's head seems stiff on her shoulders. She doesn't turn around. Chelle rubs her fist absently into her gut to quell the burning there.

Callie's tequila bottle lands on the counter with a 'thunk'. The clerk looks at Callie's ID, then back up at her.

"It's expired."

"Oh, well I can take care of that tomorrow—"

"This don't look like you." The clerk, a man in his late sixties, eyes Callie. Chelle moves a step forward.

"Excuse me, I can get it. I know her." Chelle places her bills on the counter as Callie backs away from the check-out and moves toward the exit.

Callie waits by the doors, not looking directly at anything. When Chelle has her purchases, they walk out together, but disconnected, as if another person walks between them.

Outside the colors of the sky have begun to mingle with the dark. A light in the parking lot buzzes on, seems to think better of it, and pops off again, leaving a shadow on Callie's face. Callie finally turns to her.

"Um, thanks. Here, let me get you some money—"

"Nah, my treat." Chelle doesn't meet her gaze; instead she closes her eyes and lets the breeze touch her face.

"Well I—I appreciate you not—ya know. So...yeah."

"Sure. I remember being nineteen. Nineteen, right?"

"Yeah. Twenty in April."

Chilled air passes between them, a rare desert breeze that only manifests between bursts of dead, arid heat. Callie wraps her arms around herself and looks toward the parking lot. Both women seem unwilling to walk away.

"You're going to drink that and stay put, right? No driving." Chelle says.

Callie's eyes flash, then soften as she nods.

"Okay, good." Chelle smiles a guarded smile. "You should...I don't know, come over and say 'hi' sometime." Chelle has a vision dancing in front of her—of Dan coming home to see his lover's daughter in their kitchen.

"I will."

They both nod and Chelle knows Callie won't. But she plans to invite her again if she gets a chance. She wants to see Dan's face. And she sees Marilyn's face in the girl.

∾

Callie grips the steering wheel until her hands are white and gray.

She had known she would see Mr. or Mrs. Shaw up close and personal some-day. They all live in the same city, same neighborhood. But so far, this close encounter was the first in four years. It leaves her in shock. Her mind flashes to her mom and Mr. Shaw—Marin's dad. She can't remember what he looks like. She can only remember where her mother had been in relation to him.

The party she planned on attending doesn't sound fun anymore. Callie had forgotten, maybe on purpose, how much Marin looked like her mother. She'd only been able to remember bits and pieces of Marin's face: her smile, her eyes, her teeth, her hair. Nothing cohesive to make up her whole being. Then she saw Mrs. Shaw, and it came screaming back to her. *What kind of friend forgets?*

Marin had shown Callie how to use tampons at thirteen. Callie remem-bers and her face warms, along with her body. The way Marin showed her, without compunction, trusting that she was just a girl—a normal girl like her. But Callie knew then, even then, she wasn't normal.

Callie shakes her head and doesn't acknowledge this because that would make her gay and she isn't gay. Marin was a *phase*, that's all. Callie likes guys. Men. She had been with so many by nineteen she can hardly remem-ber all of their names.

A fucking machine.

Still…girls held a mystical fascination that had Callie's mouth water-ing, her panties moistening. She squirms and wants to turn back around to the liquor store to find Marin's mom, just to see her, solidify Marin's image in her mind.

I know where Mrs. Shaw lives. Where Marin had lived.

Callie sits at the intersection too long and she hears a honk behind her. She guns the gas, sailing the car across the road and flips a U-turn before she gets to the turn off on Lake Mead Parkway. She heads back, toward home. But instead of home, she hangs a left.

Tonight she can just drive by Marin's house.

∽

At long last the house is still and then Dan remembers that since Marin died it's always still. He wonders if he thinks too much about it and if Chelle's right. She thinks Dan won't let Marin's spirit rest because all he does is think about her and talk about her.

But it isn't true. Ever since he had the talk with Marilyn that night long ago, he's let Marin go more and more. He doesn't admit to himself that he's let her go because he's afraid she judges him for fucking Marilyn; he's afraid Marin watches them from wherever she is and detests him.

He berates himself out loud.

It's nonsense and he knows it. He's become an atheist since her death. He could picture her disappearing into nothingness, but as a suicide, she'd be in Hell and he would rather her be nowhere than there.

The door opens in the kitchen and he almost scissor-kicks up off of the couch, heart pounding. He and Chelle are waking dreams, corresponding in silent gestures but never making sense.

He doesn't want to hurt her.

He already has.

She knows, and it's the one thing they don't talk about because her father did it and her mother stayed. Her mother stayed because she didn't speak the language well. She stayed out of fear.

He doesn't know why Chelle stays.

He walks into the kitchen as the door closes behind her.

"Hey." Chelle places the box on the table. Dan sees all the booze and looks at the wine rack.

"Nowhere to put that," he says.

"I can put them downstairs."

"We have a lot of wine."

"I plan on drinking more."

He's silent and watches her movements quicken, her eyes blink rapidly. She yanks thre bottles out of the box and the sound of them on the counter grows louder and louder.

"Did you eat?"

Chelle glances up at him, eyes dark. "No. I didn't get to eat."

"Me either. Maybe we could go for a run, come home, and juice something."

"I started smoking again." She walks around the counter and pulls down a wine glass, not offering him one. He knows she doesn't run. He knows she doesn't juice. She used to laugh, roll her eyes, and now she answers his questions literally.

"You shouldn't smoke. You know it makes your teeth yellow and you have lovely teeth."

"It's also bad for your health, I've heard. But it feels good."

"Oh yeah, that health thing. Speaking of, how about we go for a run—"

"I hate running. You go for a fucking run."

"I can't. I started smoking, too."

"Sure you did."

"What? I can smoke."

"Right. Last time you tried you coughed up a lung."

"Yeah, I'm still looking for that. Have you seen it?"

"No." The wine cork pops and she grabs the bottle and the glass and brushes by him.

"You taking that wine to bed with you?"

"It could be worse," she says, not turning around.

"I don't think that wine's old enough to sleep with."

He hears only silence as the bedroom door closes. He walks to her purse and finds her cigarettes. They crumble in the box as he grinds them up in his fist over the trash can.

෨

They don't kiss.

They only touch each other's bodies with their hands and Cliff stares down at his wife and can't find her anywhere.

Her eyes remain closed, her lips part slightly; Cliff is used to this. If only he could get hard.

The shower was hot and steam floats around them as they step out. He dries her off and leads her to the bed where he waits for her to situate herself, pillows under her wet head. He knows this kills her—dinner is ready downstairs, and it will be ruined. He enjoys making her suffer while he has her. It seems fitting.

She doesn't know he knows.

He kneels between her legs and she closes her eyes again, her head lulling to the side. This is the sign that she's ready to be pleasured and he wonders when that became his job. He clicks off the bedside lamp and the glow from the street out front bathes her body in a dim light.

He imagines Chelle there, dark and writhing, thick and so... *woman,* and he stirs. He's hard enough to enter Marilyn and as he does, she sighs, a small noise, like a kitten. He moves over her and she remains still. All the while he thinks of the other woman, the one who he tried to fuck but couldn't. He glides slowly into Marilyn, and out again, and in again, and wonders what Chelle's perfume had been.

He closes his eyes and kisses his wife's neck. He holds the vision of the other woman while this one takes him in. This woman who had been a cock tease until their wedding day when, before she donned her white gown, she let him finger fuck her until she came. He wonders if he's doomed to think of one while he's with the other, forever.

Marilyn sighs more audibly and he chances a look at her. Her eyes are pressed shut as if she watches a horror film scene. He wants to ask her where she is but she stopped answering him long ago, mostly because she said he didn't listen. He does listen, he just doesn't know how to prove it.

Her eyes are closed.

Is she thinking of him?

Her eyes are closed.

He slaps her flesh with his and he's rough, because he wants her to know he's here and he's with her and taking her.

Her eyes are closed.

He can't look anywhere but at her face now as pressure builds, so he slows, hoping it isn't too late and it isn't.

He moves rhythmically, wanting her eyes to fly open with the awareness that she's about to lose all control, all decorum, and then his eyes move to the wall so he doesn't come. But when he looks back at her, her eyes are open. She stares off to the right, and she brings her thumb up to her mouth to gnaw on her thumbnail.

Suddenly he can't be done soon enough. He pumps harder, his gaze moving back to the wall, back to the visions in his head. And then it's his turn to close his eyes.

5

Marilyn opens the door to a remotely familiar face.

"Hi, Mrs. Erickson, how are you? My name is Ellie Thomas, if you don't remember."

Of course she did. Ellie did a piece in the *Green Valley Review* on Callie and Marin. It was about suicide pacts. The story had been televised. How could Marilyn forget the woman's pseudo-concern as she followed them from place to place, humiliating them? Marilyn fixes her eyes on the reporter and says nothing.

"I tried calling your home phone but it was out of service."

"Yes, we had to change the number."

"I'm sorry. May I come in?"

Marilyn shakes her head, wary and cold. "This isn't a good time."

"I know what you're thinking, but just give me *five minutes.*"

Marilyn turns to look into her front room. The prospect of closing the door on the journalist and greeting the silence leaves her forlorn. After a moment, she nods.

"Alright."

The journalist steps into the house and Marilyn already regrets it as the woman's eyes search every inch of her massive front room.

"Shall we sit?"

"That's fine." Marilyn indicates the couch; she chooses a chair across from it and places her hands between her knees.

"I'm doing a follow-up piece on your daughter. Sort of a 'life affirming' story, to help kids see that suicide is not an option. I also understand you volunteer for YSPC. You must—"

"I'm not sure what you want from us."

"Well, for starters, how have the past four years been?"

Marilyn opens her mouth and can't make noise. How have the past four years been?

The back door opens and Marilyn turns to see Callie stumble into the hallway near the front room.

"Callie, you're home."

The journalist stands. "Hi, Callie, I'm—"

"I'm sorry, I can't meet anyone right now. I have homework!" Callie's face reflects dazed joy and Marilyn stands and briskly walks toward her. Marilyn can smell the smoke.

"Well," Marilyn smiles tightly, "There's your life affirming story," she says under her breath.

Callie's brow furrows. "Life what?"

"Nothing."

The reporter walks half-way to where Callie stands and offers her hand. "I'm Ellie. Do you remember me?"

Callie's eyes flit to the side and her chin drops. "No. Should I? Oh, I know, you're from the garden club and you've come to complain about our ugly landscaping." Callie giggles.

"She did the story on you four years ago." Marilyn takes her seat again, eyes weary.

"Oh, right." Callie walks past Ellie and sits in the other arm chair, mimicking Marilyn's posture. "So what? I mean...what?" She shrugs.

"Well," Ellie begins, taking her seat on the couch, "you must be in college by now, how are you feeling about that?"

"Wow," Callie laughs, "this is like therapy. I feel fan-fucking-tastic. How do *you* feel?"

Marilyn's head snaps toward her daughter. "Callie—"

Callie smiles a lop-sided grin. "Sorry. Okay, so it's great. Yeah. So glad I'm not, ya know...dead."

"Oh my God, Callie," Marilyn shuts her eyes.

"What, mom? She obviously wants to do some sort of—"

"Maybe this is a bad time." Ellie stands.

Callie holds out both hands to her. "No! It's a great time. See, after class, we sit around and I'm all, 'I'm so happy I'm alive.' Is that right? Can you print that?"

"Jesus." Marilyn places her fingers above her eye in a distressed salute. "I'm…sorry."

"No, it's fine. I'll come another time." Ellie is already half-way to the front door.

"Bye!" Callie waves and holds back laughter as the front door closes firmly.

Marilyn stays seated, hunched over. The carpet swirls mesmerize her and it's suddenly peaceful. Callie might as well have been far away.

"Wow, she was touchy."

Marilyn shifts her gaze from the carpet to her daughter and stares at her with searching eyes. Wanting to understand, wanting to reach out and smooth her hair away from her face, she wants to move closer. But she doesn't know how to touch her. She can't touch her.

Callie finally stands. "Well, I have homework."

Marilyn can't seem to move, speak. She waits for Callie's bedroom door to shut and only then do the carpet swirls pull her back into her trance.

෨

The man at the front counter looks vaguely familiar. Cliff realizes he's a former patient.

"Do I know you?"

Cliff smiles. "I'm not from around here."

"You must have one of those faces."

"Yes, I think I do. Room—?"

"Fifteen. Other side, top floor."

Cliff nods and walks back out to the car. Chelle has leaned her seat back. She has a headache. Her full breasts undulate slightly when the car moves.

After Cliff parks, the silence causes his mouth to go dry. He opens the car door but stays seated.

"How's your head?"

"I drank too much wine last night."

"Sorry. You want me to get you some aspirin?"

"No, I'll be okay." She waits for him to come around and open her door.

They mount the dirty steps, concrete, in disrepair, one by one. The motel isn't as obvious as the former hotel they'd visited—one of the nicer hotels in Henderson. Cliff wants to be careful. Then he sees the guy at the check-in. *Jesus.*

His shoes strike each step with a thud, reverberating up his leg. He glances past his shoes, past the stairs and takes in Chelle's heels, legs, her ass, supple and round. Her hips sway with each step; there's nothing bony about her.

At the top of the stairs he places his hand on her elbow and guides her along the walkway. He puts her in front of him to hide himself. She isn't anyone's podiatrist.

As they enter, Cliff scans behind him once more.

The smoky room is pitch dark except the small ray of light from the open door. The sanitizer smell mingles to create a homogenized ashtray. He doesn't want to open his mouth to breathe but he does anyway. He wants to be there a while.

Chelle places her bag on the floor and lies down on the bedspread. The spread is plain gold, rough, and smoke-infused. He sniffs harder and detects urine.

"Come here." Cliff pulls down the covers and the sheets are blindingly white. He touches Chelle's soft hand and is surprised at the effect it has on him. She moves over to the white sheets and smiles at him. Cliff doesn't undress. He moves above her and lays the length of her. They kiss and the sweet shudder of arousal causes him to plunge his tongue into her mouth. She returns his fervor, moaning and raising her hips.

As she unbuttons her jeans, Cliff stands and helps her wriggle them down her thighs. Her full legs, soft and curvaceous, are so different from his wife's. Marilyn's legs are twigs. There's sinew and bone and tendons and nothing to sink into and Chelle's thighs have to be parted to see between her legs. He pulls off her panties. They are moist and he resists the urge to bring them to his nose, but he wants to. He wants a preview, a scent to come home to when he kneels before her.

He kneels on the floor, the carpet rough on his knees, and begins kissing her inner thighs. He unzips his pants and works his cock free. Her hands tangle in his hair.

He sees red. Dark red moistening her opening. It trickles down her and he stops. He wants to bury his head there, but the blood stops him and he glances up at her.

"Oh God, am I bleeding?"

"Yes. It's alright, though, we can just—" he moves to get up.

"No, don't. I want you to stay right there."

Chelle reaches down and her finger slides between her legs. Cliff sits back on his heels, mesmerized. She moves her fingers and he watches and nothing happens between his legs but it feels like it does because he's ready to come.

He's still soft, but watching, he squeezes his barely full cock and it causes him to gasp.

Her eyes don't leave him, but a musky shadow infuses them as her fingers explore, careful not to touch the crimson trickle of blood. Cliff thinks back and realizes he's never seen this, never watched a woman pleasure herself this close, this intimately. The blood takes it deeper into the forbidden, to a place in him that hungers to cover himself with it. This thought along with one final stroke causes him to cry out, shuddering, grasping her supple thigh.

Her fingers slow and stop. Chelle removes her hand but Cliff takes hold of her wrist. "You can keep going."

"No. I'm okay." Her eyes are soft and she rolls over. "Hand me my pants?"

Cliff still gasps for air, his chest like fire, his belly vibrating. "Sorry. I'm—"

"No, don't be sorry. I liked it."

Chelle reaches for him. He moves up her body. Kissing her softly, he brings his hand to her face. They touch foreheads and Cliff meets her gaze. His expression turns blank, like a switch is thrown.

"I slept with her last night. I...just thought you should know."

Chelle's face changes slightly. "Oh yeah? How was that." Her dark eyes glitter just a little.

"I don't know. I—I love her."

Her hand touches his hair, smoothing it back from his forehead and she blinks and shrugs.

"Of course you do. She's your wife."

ॐ

Chelle slumps down in the car feigning a head ache. She knows no one will see her through Cliff's tinted windows. She doesn't want to be seen by anyone—not even strangers at this cheap hole.

Cliff looks frazzled as he comes back to the car. He'd spoken to the hotel clerk a little longer than she would have imagined him to. Did Cliff know him?

"How's your head?" Cliff asks.

"Still hurts. It's my own fault. I never drink that much."

"Did Dan and you share a bottle?"

She turns her head toward him. "No. I was alone."

He nods, making a mild frowning gesture with his mouth as if to imply only mild, detached curiosity.

"Why did you ask?" she says.

"I just wanted to know. That's all."

When they park, she is conscious of the open parking spaces surrounding them, the air touching every part of her; the air has eyes. The air sees into her.

Cliff is more nervous this time and it's contagious—she can't stop glancing behind them, either.

The room smells rancid, and she plops on the bed, exhausted. Her stomach rumbles with hunger and something more. It's time for her period to start. Her period has become this unpredictable, sentient thing, as if revisiting her from adolescence, coming at the worst possible times and in varying degrees of severity.

One day she could hardly leave the house; it soaked through her pads and her tampons just dropped out. She doubled up her night-time pads and lay in bed, sleeping and feeling the blood seep from her as if slowly dying.

The only time bleeding like that made sense was when Marin was born. The blood never stopped. Fragrant and rust-red, it was as alive as the dark-haired infant who suckled at her breast. Chelle closes her eyes and opens them, seeing Cliff and focusing on him.

He lays on top of her and she still smells the fragrant blood and hears her daughter cry and wants to bolt from this cheap room. But she can't. He's here and they had agreed without words to finish it, somehow bring the pain full-circle. It's as if they want to throw two elements together in a test tube to see what it will make, what kind of catastrophe they can conjure.

The room had been so dark that Cliff spread the heavy drapes to reveal gauzy white curtains. She and Cliff remove her pants and she curses the curtains and their lack of opacity as sun filters through the white with holy fire, lighting her body like a tree in morning.

Then Cliff tells her there's blood.

Of course there has to be blood. There has to be blood because she is bleeding and it shows only in the place that is open, the place she can open for him. For them.

He loves Marilyn. Dan loves Marilyn. Chelle bleeds.

ભ

Callie hears moaning which is only strange for a moment because then she dreams. It's a fitful, waking dream brought on by too many pills, too much alcohol. Too much pot. Her nostrils itch and she can't move her arm high enough to wipe away the strange, alive sensation in them.

Dust lines her mouth like a cloak and she's so thirsty, so hot. Her legs shiver and jump while sweat trickles in an aggravating stream between her breasts.

She hears someone talking and tries to move her tongue, tries to ask for water. She opens her eyes and the room is on its side, blurry and brown. She imagines her mother is there but then she sees Marin in her mind and wants it to be her so she can save her.

As if Marin could save her from herself. As if she would.

Noises come from behind her and it's only then she notices she is curled next to Josh's friend—what's his name? *Nathan.* His name is Nathan. *No wonder I'm so hot.*

As she lays prostrate, she moves her chin up and to the right to see what's behind her. Josh lazily dry humps some girl in the corner. Her name escapes Callie, but she remembers she brought the good weed.

Light drizzles through an upper window in the small warehouse with its dust and bottles littering the floor. The particles of dust are alive and Callie holds her breath for a brief second before her head spins.

Nathan's arm lifts and flops onto her and she rolls out from under it. She barely has the strength to wave away his hands. He caresses her ass and his hand moves between her legs. She moves incrementally away now, her mouth tasting like turpentine and chemicals, her eyes crusted with the dust of the room. Callie's stomach churns with the thought of him sprawling the length of her.

She sits up and the screaming pain in her head almost causes her stomach to lurch and lose everything. Up against the far wall bodies sprawl out like the dead and lie in disarray while in the other corner, potheads wake and bake to some hot-knifed hash.

As abruptly as a slap, the rays of the sun hit the window and a couple of people yelp in protest. Callie crawls on her hands and knees and sits alone in the middle of a pile of blankets. She remembers being cold last night. The nights are getting colder.

Footsteps behind her and her head won't obey. She wants to see who approaches; her back feels exposed and the spins have started.

Cold plastic on her shoulder. Her hand reaches for it before she sees the person standing behind her. Callie grasps the bottle, the paper on the label wet and disintegrating with her fingers. It's orange. Orange juice. Callie can't move her head or the spins will overtake her.

Jeans, ripped and covered with ink and words, come into her view. Black boots with scuff marks on them. Her eyes elevator up slowly to a ragged-edged t-shirt that reads "Misfits". Breasts, round and full, swell behind the shirt, straining against the black cloth.

The girl's arms are tattooed, along with her upper chest. There's a ring in her lip and a smirk on her full mouth. Her spiky two-toned hair covers half of her face.

"Well, if it isn't Miss Suburb."

"What?"

The girl folds her legs under her like she is made of liquid and sits in front of Callie. "I called you that last night. Remember?"

Callie shakes her head almost imperceptibly.

"I asked you what a nice, suburban girl was doing in a place like this? You told me you were doing charity work because you're *Miss Suburb?* You don't remember *any* of this?"

Callie squeezes her eyes shut. She remembers puking outside. It had been cold.

"Oh, well shit then." The girl smiles and drapes both arms over her knees. "Do you even remember my name?"

Callie shakes her head.

"Ryanne. *Ryanne.* Jeez."

"What's my name?" Callie stares at her. Ryanne moves her eyes to the side, then back to Callie.

"Miss Suburb!"

Callie smiles and tries to open her orange juice.

"Here, let me." Ryanne reaches for the bottle and opens it effortlessly. "What's your name? Tell me."

"Callie. I don't remember *shit.*"

"No kidding you don't. Remember him?" She points to Nathan, curled up on the floor on a foam pad.

Callie groans.

"Yeah, I'd groan too. And go get fucking tested."

"Did I use a condom?"

Ryanne suddenly has a sour look on her face. "Am I your fucking mother? How the fuck should I know?"

Callie's hand trembles as she lifts the bottle to her lips. Ryanne looks away sullenly, then back to Callie. "What are you doing here?"

"Charity work."

Ryanne stares at her for a while, then breaks into a grin, revealing straight white teeth. "You want to go home?"

"Not yet. I need sleep, or food, or I need to puke."

"Come with me." Ryanne helps her up and they walk, stepping gingerly over Nathan's sleeping body.

Ryanne doesn't let go of her hand.

6

Her hand is warm and dry. Callie keeps the hand Ryanne holds passive as Ryanne leads her past bodies lying on foam pads and coats. With her other hand Ryanne softly slaps metal poles as she passes them. The paint on them is peeling, revealing rust and dull gray metal and Callie wants to touch them, too, but her hand is in Ryanne's and she doesn't want to let her go.

"Where are we going?"

"Relax. I didn't give you O.J. just to lure you away and kill you."

"Funny." The sentiment causes the juice to turn acidic in Callie's stomach.

There is a small structure inside the warehouse, like a miniature one-story office building. The dark hallway at the center leads to four partitioned offices. Ryanne steps into the dark doorway and Callie follows.

"This your first time at dock thirteen, huh?"

"Yeah. Dock thirteen?"

Ryanne shrugs. "They say thirteen people died here in industrial accidents, so they closed it down."

"Seriously?" Callie moves faster and her eyes dart toward the closed doors. The sunlight from the main warehouse barely illuminates them.

Ryanne cocks and eyebrow. "Hell yeah. Didn't you hear about it?"

"No—"

Ryanne's smile spreads and Callie yanks her hand down, out of her grasp. "You *bitch*!"

Ryanne laughs delightedly. "Yes I am. C'mon."

Callie's face burns, and her stomach still flutters from fear. She berates herself for trusting this *Ryanne* person when she is so clearly *fucked up.*

Ryanne stops at the last door in the structure and pushes hard. "A little help here?"

The thick rubber strip underneath the door has come loose and blocks it. Callie pushes with her and the door struggles open. Ryanne flips on the light which, mercifully, consists of only one humming, faint bulb.

The room is empty except for a desk and an old quilt.

"You don't live here, do you?" Callie's face registers disdain as walks toward the desk.

"I have an apartment. But my roommate's a preppy bitch. Like you."

"I'm *not* preppy and I—" Ryanne peers at her under half-closed eyelids. Callie's aware suddenly of her flowing, lustrous hair and American Eagle shirt. "Whatever, I hate labels."

"Why is it that people hate labels only when other people label them correctly?"

Callie wracks her brain for something intelligent to say. "Thanks, Dr. Freud. You're dead, you know."

Ryanne doesn't react. Humming to herself, she removes a wall panel and pulls out a shallow box. Callie sees packages.

"Okay, we got a blueberry Danish, a cream cheese one, two apple, 'cause they're my favorite and I buy a lot of them...let's see, Snickers, Ding Dongs..."

"I'll take an apple Danish."

"See? Preppy bitch, taking my shit."

"Whatever, you offered it." Callie scowls a little.

"You need to unclench."

She hands it to Callie whose stomach grumbles and stabs at her. The plastic crinkles in her hand and when she opens it, the pastry smell is rich and cloying.

"I like apple. I liked it before I even met you."

"I'm just *teasing.*" Ryanne slides down the wall and opens her package with two fingers and her thumbs as if the plastic is soiled. Callie watches her fingers work, long and refined, with a narrow-ish palm that makes them seem younger than their owner.

Callie sits across from her and they eat in silence.

"Thanks for the food and juice."

"Sure."

"So what...where did you get your name?"

"My mom and dad."

Callie tips her head with an irritated look on her face and Ryanne laughs. "Sorry, I'm a smart ass."

"Whatever."

"No, I got it from them because I was supposed to be a boy."

"Oh, yeah?"

"It's not like I don't try to be one," Ryanne smiles and takes another bite.

Callie watches Ryanne's arms. The inked images on them look alive, as if they twirl. She feels her head and vision swim.

"I don't feel so good." Callie moves to stand.

"Here, lie down. I'll find some water."

Callie lies on the carpet and soon, the quilt is under her head as Ryanne tucks it gently around her neck. Its musty odor is comforting. Callie glances up, already feeling a bit better.

"I need to go home."

Ryanne smiles and moves her hair from her face. "Sure you do, Miss Suburb. I'll bet there are people there who miss you."

๑๑

Dan's lunch break consists of a meatloaf sandwich and a Coke. He leans against the waist-high sand stone wall in front of St. Thomas Catholic Church. It's the closest he's been to church in almost four years.

He tells himself he's defying the concept of God by eating a meatloaf sandwich here on a Thursday afternoon. He hasn't seen Marilyn in four days. The meatloaf dries in his mouth and he chugs the cold soda and swallows heavily.

Worshipers file by and he turns his back toward them, not wanting to insult them with his chosen lunch locale. He's only here to insult God.

The big wooden door at the top of the stairs opens and closes with a rush of cool air, and Dan can't help but turn to watch. His eyes are met by Father Britton. Dan utters a heart-felt curse under his breath.

The priest nods and greets the last parishioner and instead of going inside, walks out into the glaring afternoon, robes flowing. Father Britton prefers the drama of the traditional cassock over the more contemporary shirt, pants, and collar. Dan sighs audibly as the priest approaches.

"Hello, Father."

"Daniel. I'm so glad you're eating here."

"Did God inspire you to come and pull me inside?"

"Oh, no, no. I'll take what I can get at this juncture."

Dan nods and takes another bite, not wanting one, but wanting his mouth full.

"How are things, Dan?"

He chews and points to his mouth, smiling. Unfortunately, the priest is patient. Finally he says:

"I couldn't be better. If I were any better, they'd have to arrest me."

"Always the joker. You've been that way since you were a kid. It's how you dealt with your mother's death, too."

Dan stops, almost takes another bite and lowers his sandwich. He looks out over the street, his face hard. "I didn't come here to confess, Father."

"I can imagine. You can, though, you know. Do you have anything to confess?"

Dan looks at him, all joking aside. "You have no idea."

The priest smiles kindly. "Come in, Dan. Confess. Relieve your soul of the burden it carries. Then come take the Eucharist and be at peace."

"I can't do that, Father."

"Why on Earth not, my son?"

"Because I can't confess something that I plan on continuing."

"I see."

Dan stands and grabs his bag. "And I can't believe in a God who would punish someone already in pain."

"It's not my law, Daniel."

"I know. And unlike most men, God can't be bribed. So God must be an unfeeling prick."

Dan's eye twitches imperceptibly at his insult. Father Britton doesn't flinch. He seems saddened by Dan and reaches out to touch his shoulder.

"My son, there is still hope yet."

"Hope for what? My own soul? I don't care about my own soul. I care about hers."

"Then come inside. Let us pray for it."

"No...I can't pray to God anymore, Father, sorry. He and I, we've parted ways."

Father Britton smiles with his lips together but his eyes are soft and sorrowful.

Dan opens his eyes wide and grabs the priests' sleeve. "Hey, Father... how many sins can I get away with and still get to heaven?"

Father Britton shakes his head and pats Dan's back. He turns and walks up the stairs.

"Seriously Father, just a number."

"Good bye, Daniel. God bless you."

"A ballpark...just a round figure..." Dan calls out.

The church door closes and Dan stares at it for a long time. He pushes away from the wall and stuffs his half-eaten sandwich into his bag as he walks toward his car.

He doesn't know why he came to church. But he feels microscopically better.

෬

His lips crush hers. Normally she loves kissing him, but tonight feels different. His arms suffocate her and his rough hands scratch at her skin.

He'd brought a blanket but it doesn't mitigate the discomfort of the hard floor on her back. It only provides a thin physical barrier to the worn carpet.

"Dan, you're smothering me."

"Sorry. I've just missed you so much." He pulls her closer. Marilyn allows him to pull her, like she allowed him to tackle her onto the floor tonight. She allows it because she still feels his pang of loss. She has lost her daughter, too. He just doesn't know it.

He pulls her shirt out from her skirt and his rough hands find her breasts, no longer full. It's as if the air has been let out of her whole body, a brittle stick.

His wandering touch is perfunctory. The main event is him sliding inside of her and she finds her legs are glued at the knees.

"What's wrong?" he asks.

"Nothing, I—Callie didn't come home last night and I worry about her, that's all."

"I'm sorry."

Marilyn hasn't told him about Callie. She hasn't mentioned the loss, the betrayal, the absentee daughter that is just as ghostly as his. It is easily argued that at least she *has* Callie. But she knows better.

Dan can't talk about her daughter. He's reminded of the hole in his life and so Marilyn usually obliges, but not today. Today she felt the need to say it out loud. Her hollow chest has worry ricocheting around like a bullet, piercing her from the inside.

Dan's touching resumes in earnest and soon Marilyn mirrors his fervor as she loses herself to the moment. She allows the need for comfort to trickle out of her as his hands invade her.

The sweet and tender love-making from a few months ago has been eclipsed by purpose: forgetting and quieting the noise. It's the way Dan and Marilyn connect now. She misses the heady heat and the control. She'd once had control. But now she can't refuse. She can only fuck.

"Wait!" Marilyn sits up on her elbows, head cocked.

"What is it?" He doesn't stop kissing her neck.

"Dan, listen."

At first there's silence. She's worried someone is inside. Then they both hear it at once.

The unmistakable ringtone of the crisis line. They freeze, listening as the sound gets louder in their silence.

"The service will get it." Dan says, unmoving.

But the ringing continues and Marilyn stares at Dan, unsure and impotent. She looks to him to act. He is frozen, too.

"It's not picking up." Mild panic in her voice and a surge of energy permeates her limbs. Is it too late?

They both move at once; she pulls her skirt down, he hoists his pants up and together they burst from the office and run down the hall.

Marilyn stops just short of the lit reception office. Dan scrambles to the other side of the desk and grabs the phone. His face is red and streaked with sweat and she can only stare at him, feeling as guilty as the day she'd found his daughter.

"Hello! Hello, I'm here! Hello!"

He continues to talk, attempting to revive the lifeless phone line, knowing no one is on the other end, not anymore.

"I'm sorry," she whispers. Her chest burns and her breathing quickens as he slowly, silently sets the phone on the receiver.

"Jesus Christ." He wipes his face with a trembling hand. The look on his face causes her to shrink from him, as if at any moment, he would visit recrimination on her.

"We didn't hear it." Her voice is hollow and he still stares at the phone. Finally he pulls out a chair and sits, waiting. As he waits, Marilyn zips up her skirt and quietly leaves for home.

ॐ

"Callie, when did you get home?"

"Hey, Dad. I've been home for a while."

"You didn't come home at all last night. Your mother and I were worried sick."

Callie pouts disingenuously. "I fell asleep at Taylor's house, Daddy."

Cliff softens. She calls him the moniker from her childhood and he forgets it all: the hurt, the ingratitude, the lies, all of it. He musters a stern face.

"A phone call, Cal. It's not rocket science, Honey. You call Mom or me and tell us where you are."

"You know I'm okay, and I—"

"How do we know you're okay?"

"I'm always okay." Her smile holds anger, irony.

"And I want to make sure you are."

"How about you? Are you okay?"

She always does this and Cliff fights it. She turns it around and soon, he's confessing to her. But not this time.

"I'm fine. That isn't the point and you know it."

"You look tired, Daddy. Maybe you should get more sleep."

He glares at her. "I would if you'd call."

"I'm not the only thing you should be losing sleep over."

Cliff swallows and his mouth dries. *She knows? How?*

"I don't know what you mean." He regrets it the second it leaves his mouth. His face burns with humiliation and he stands straighter, taller. She can't see him like this.

Callie shrugs. "I just think you and Mom need to talk more."

"Mom and I are fine, Pumpkin. You don't have to worry about that."

"I'm not a fucking five year old."

"And I am your father! Watch your mouth!"

Her eyes open wide. He never yells.

"Sorry, Dad. Jeez, I just worry. Mom's losing weight, you're looking, well...old—"

"Your mother and I are getting old, and get older every time you don't come home!"

"So it's my fault you're aging?"

"I didn't mean it that—"

"Great, heap some more guilt on me. Have I caused you to go blind, maybe given you herpes because I didn't come home? Jesus!"

"Callie, c'mon, stop. You know that isn't what I meant. I just want you to be okay."

"And I want you to be okay, Dad. But you have to, you know...talk to Mom."

"About what, Callie?"

She's silent and he sees her eyes as they search the room for anything she can use to fill the gaps. He will deny anything. He lifts his chin. He can deny it; it would be easy.

"She spends too much time at The Center, Dad. You know it and I know it."

He holds her gaze for a long time. His absorption is like a heartbeat: timed, alive, soothing. He could stare at his daughter all day and only see her as the small golden-haired little girl, the little girl who called him Daddy.

7

The dough is soft, malleable. Chelle kneads it and pulls it up to her face again to smell it. Mouth watering, she presses it back down on the marble board and uses her palms to flatten it out. She takes another bite of carrot.

"Dammit!" Her lower, inner lip is bloody from her biting it every time she eats. She chews carefully, her lip throbbing and raw.

All is right with the world if she makes the dough perfectly round, as if she's pleasing her mother up in heaven.

That's good, Mija, good, make it perfect and round, just like an angel.

Her mother is easier to talk to now that she's in heaven. On Earth her mother was always nervous and afraid. Chelle would talk to her and if she had anything bad to say, she would end up having to comfort Manuela, not the other way around.

Her fingers deftly find the spots that need smoothing. But she can't seem to smooth anything out anymore. The dough is mocking her. She pulls it up and balls it again.

Too warm.

She picks up another dough sphere and works it, the soothing sensation escaping her as she hears the clock chime eleven. The dough refuses to conform, and she uses her whole hand to flatten it into submission. *You are the dough, I am the cook. You will do as I say.* Another bite of carrot yields another expletive.

Outside, her dog, Bowser barks. She goes to the window and sees his tail wagging, his ears perked. He can sense when Dan is near. She slaps the dough down again and works it, the oil in the pan getting impatient and smoky.

When the door opens, Chelle jumps with a start even though she had heard him coming.

"Cooking?" Dan asks.

"Where were you."

"I toldja I worked late tonight."

Dan walks over and stops short of a tentative embrace as she flinches. Chelle sucks her bottom lip.

"What's wrong?"

"I'm in pain."

"I'm sorry," he says, moving closer.

"Par for the course." She shows him her inner lip.

"What happened?" He asks.

"I've been biting my lip all week."

"Why don't you stop?"

"Because if I stop, that means I don't talk. I stay silent."

"So you're doomed to bite your lip."

"Not your fault."

"Doesn't mean I like to see you in pain."

Chelle places the dough in the oil and turns away from her husband. The dough in the pan is perfectly round, just like an angel.

☙

The cup's condensation drips on Callie's bare legs. She pulls the lid off of the cup and stares into it, squinting.

"Is that fruit?"

"Yeah, it's red wine jungle juice from my parents' party last night." Ryanne takes another swig. "I tried to not get fruit in the cup. Sorry. Drink slower, Suburb, or you'll get sick."

Callie chews on a dark purple pineapple chunk. "Mmm, I like the fruit. What are we doing here anyway? Cemeteries are creepy."

"I like them better than parks."

"Let's go to the warehouse or—"

"Nah. Leave your drink and come with me. Let's walk."

Callie doesn't want to appear afraid. She slurps the last of her cup and belches. "'Scuse me."

"You're gonna be sick."

"No I won't. It's not the first time I've had alcohol."

"Whatever you say. So what about that guy from the other night?"

"What about him?"

"You with him or what?"

"Fuck no. I just got drunk and we fucked. It's no big deal."

Ryanne cocks an eyebrow at her. "Why is fucking not a big deal?"

"It just isn't."

"You hetero chicks are fucked up."

"Oh, but you lesbians are *so* together." Callie rolls her eyes.

"So you figured me out."

"The rainbow earrings were sort of a dead giveaway. Oh, sorry, a *real* giveaway." Callie points to the cemetery sign and snickers. "Don't want to piss off anyone."

"I think the people here are beyond pissed off, unlike you."

"What's that supposed to mean?"

"You're always pissy. Or mad."

"'Always'? You've known me for what, three days?"

"Yeah, and you're always pissy."

"Whatever." Callie stumbles faster along the path and Ryanne jogs to keep up.

"Hey, Suburb, where you going? I'm the leader, remember?"

"Just walking." The evening air hugs her and she moves as if pulled by invisible strings. Her legs remind her of a child's legs at recess, when their legs move too fast for them to control.

Ryanne speeds up to her and grabs her hand. "Hold up! Jesus. Where are you going, anyway?"

"Nowhere. Just over to that bench. I wanna go *over there*."

Callie knows the general area because her mother had told her where it is. She'd never been here. Being drunk and in this place is perfect; she wants to fly. Callie twirls with out—stretched arms and laughs, looking up. When the sky continues to spin she stops and holds her hands out. Ryanne grabs her.

"You're crazy, Suburb."

"And you're a crazy urban…goddess." Callie's speech slurs a little.

"Whatever. I live in Henderson, not Vegas."

"It's close enough." Callie releases Ryanne's hand and wanders near the bench toward the graves, searching the markers until, at last, the familiar name appears in front of her eyes, as if an artifact has been unearthed. Callie clears her throat and reads aloud. *Marin Manuela Shaw. Nineteen ninety-one to two thousand-six.*"

"Why are you reading that?" Ryanne stands close, shivering a little.

"I knew her."

"You *knew* her?"

"Yeah, I knew her." Callie walks to the nearby concrete bench and straddles it, her back to the grave. "She was my best friend."

"Oh, *shit*."

"It was forever ago."

Ryanne stares wide-eyed at the marker, then moves over and mirrors Callie on the bench. "We can go if you—"

She doesn't finish because Callie grabs the back of her neck, pulls her in and plants a deep, open-mouthed kiss on her lips.

Ryanne responds with her own mouth, but then she pushes Callie away. "What are you doing?"

"I'm showing my best friend that I'm over her. You got that, Marin? *I'm over you!*" Callie stares up, her throat pale and slender.

Ryanne's eyes show too much white as she stares at Callie. Cars run across gravel behind a fence near them and Callie's gaze penetrate Ryanne's. Callie leans in closer.

"People are coming. Why don't you hurry and fuck me." Callie places Ryanne's hand on her chest.

Ryanne pulls her hand gently away. "I don't fuck drunk. I especially don't fuck drunk, straight girls...look, there are so many things fucked up with this picture, I can't even *begin* to tell you."

Callie opens her legs wider and Ryanne's gaze falls to Callie's skirt.

"Please..."

Ryanne's mouth is open. She swallows and shakes her head. "C'mon, let's get outta here. C'mon, Suburb."

Ryanne lifts her leg and stands. As she walks away Callie calls after her. "Chicken shit!" Callie looks at the grave marker as the insult reverberates through the night and back into her ears.

∽

He's called her four times. That's enough. He knows he shouldn't have been so obsessive about that caller at The Center. He kicks himself now. Marilyn is not the type of woman to keep waiting.

Dan sits in the garage and the stink of oil and gasoline make his throat raw. The oil stains make Rorschach blots on the ground and he sees himself in them, a blackened mirror. He is half tempted to go to her house, but her pale, stiff husband would be there.

His work boot steps on the oil stain and he stares, trying to configure it into a familiar form. The only shape it seems to take for him is the essence of an unblinking eye. He pulls his fingers through his curly black hair, leaving it mussed and at attention from the constant raking.

Chelle isn't home yet. He wonders if she's working late again. His momentary worry about Marilyn is eclipsed by his wife. For a brief moment. His wife has black eyes that are black ice and flint and there's that hole again he feels when he thinks of her. That hole that can't ever be filled because their daughter is gone and any chances of any more are gone with her. He feels Chelle's presence in the box of holiday knick-knacks on the shelf in front of him.

His mother would have called it a sin. Adultery: an ugly, venial sin. But there's nothing in him to connect to that word anymore. *Marilyn* is synonymous with *love* and isn't that the highest commandment of all?

Then he calls again.

"Hi, Mar...baby, I know I'm not supposed to leave messages...God. I'm so sorry about the other night. I miss you. Please call me. Uhh...just call me when you can. I'm heading into work in a bit, so you can call me—"

He runs out of time.

ᖇᖇ

The cold granite counter top sticks to her icy hands as if they are long lost friends. The smooth, rounded edge fits perfectly in her palm as Marilyn gazes out the back window at the shimmering water of their swimming pool.

When Cliff and she bought the house, Callie and she had begged him, swore oaths to him, that the pool would never go unused. Marilyn keeps her end of the bargain by merely skimming the surface with the net and closing the cover at night so snakes don't get in. Beyond the pool is her ever-growing garden project. She's allowed it to overgrow, and now the symmetry is off. The Red Yucca has eclipsed the Mexican Bird of Paradise and she can hardly see the Lantana ground cover.

Her phone vibrates on the counter, sending chills through her. She can almost feel the vibrations travel through the granite and into her fingers. But that makes no sense; granite wouldn't carry the movement into her hands. The phone continues to ring, and with each vibration her heart rate ramps up a notch. Mercifully, it becomes still.

Pushing herself back from the counter, she reaches for her porcelain drawer handle, bright in cobalt blue and white, and takes out the kitchen shears.

The steel is cold on her thigh as she moves toward the back door. She knows she ought to use the garden shears, but the garage feels far away. On the other side of the world.

The scorching air outside immediately crushes her lungs, even though a breeze wiggles the palms and leaves. She can almost feel the water from the pool on her face, encompassing her body. A brief visual of Cliff's naked body before they turn out the pool lights. They don't swim naked anymore.

Marilyn attacks the Yucca and watches the stalks fall. It is the time of year, she reasons, to cut it all out, get it ready for a winter death. Although in Nevada, nothing every truly dies in winter; the last notable exception was in 2004. That snow fall dumped white fluff over every protesting palm, cactus, and lawn.

Marilyn looks up knowing snow, if it ever revisits, won't come for three months yet. But she wants it now—that pure breath of fresh air that cleans the lungs and naturally prunes the Earth.

The flowers and stalks lay at her feet and she stoops to gather them. The garden is devoid of color now, and as she looks at the healthy stalks lying on the ground, Marilyn's nose burns and tears gather in her eyes.

She weeps because when she stood at the window, she thought she had been staring at the pool, when really her eyes had been captivated by the color of the flowers all along.

She doesn't go to the garage; she walks into the house, her arms filled with twigs and greens and dying flora. She lays the colorful orphans on the marble and seeks a vase from the upper cupboard. The glass on the vase she plucks from the shelf is smooth and cold, like granite, and she fills it with water. As she places the snipped plants in the vase, she realizes there won't be enough room in it for all of them.

She doesn't know which bunches to throw away, so she finds more vases.

Soon, they stand in a row, like a procession of protesters at a rally. She pulls and fluffs and twists, but they all have minds of their own. The flora rests in the vases as a mass of weeds. No matter what she does, they are weeds.

She can't throw them out, and yet she can't bear to look at them another second.

8 _____

She insists that he wash his hands when he gets home. Cliff even has a sink in his office. He stands at it now, scouring his nails.

It's maddening because he washes them between each patient. Marilyn doesn't like feet. They used to have good-natured arguments about how feet are cleaner than mouths, and how Cliff should perhaps have trained in dentistry.

She would have preferred he had done surgical residency.

He had explained to her the extensive hours he would be gone and now that he knows her, it makes more sense.

A short, sharp knock at the door. He knows his assistant's knock by heart.

"Yes, Heidi?" Her round face appears in the doorway.

"Dr. Erickson, Mrs. Hellen wants to know if she can wait until next month to get her orthotics—"

"That's fine, but tell her that I want to see her six weeks after she starts wearing them. So adjust the appointment to that."

"Okay, thanks." Heidi quickly closes the door to his office and he inhales her familiar perfume. She always wears one spray too much.

She's been on his staff for thirteen years and never once has he asked her anything personal. She has never asked him. But she has a maternal quality that makes him want to seek out her wisdom, even though he never has. In fact, she has run his office expertly for ten years and he feels in awe of her most of the time.

But he is the doctor.

He dries his hands briskly on a rough paper towel and walks to his desk.

Heidi brings treats on Fridays. She tells him of her newest grandchild. She had covered for everything when he'd taken the week off four years ago to sit by Callie in the hospital after her overdose.

That's what he calls it: an over-dose, as if Callie had nothing to do with it. As if Marilyn and he had nothing to do with it.

It was an over-*dose*.

A cry for help.

He cries for help. He turns to Chelle and when she opens her legs for him, he can't give her any part of him. Marilyn had opened her heart to him once and he couldn't give anything to her either. Now, both are closed and he is still closed and it feels like nothing could open to him again.

Cliff walks to his sink and washes his hands again. He can, at the very least, give Marilyn that.

❦

Chelle moves and the paper under her crackles. She looks at her feet in the stirrups and realizes it's time for a pedicure. She reflexively straightens her toes and curls them as they slowly begin to freeze in the frigid room.

Instinctively she moves her butt toward the edge of the exam table. He'll tell her to do that anyway, even though her body initially rebels and stays as far from his hands as possible.

She can feel the trickle of blood down her inner thigh. It irritates her and tickles, but before she can grab a tissue, there's a rap at the door and it opens with a *whoosh*.

"Chelle, how are you?" Dr. Montaigne is accompanied by a new nurse and she smiles perfunctorily.

"Embarrassed. I'm bleeding again, I'm sorry—I thought I was done."

"No worries." The doctor grabs a tissue, scoots his chair up to Chelle and lifts the white drape, dabbing at her thigh. "So the bleeding hasn't let up?"

"Well, it's sporadic."

"Since the procedure?"

"Yes."

"Has it been every month?"

"Yes, really heavy bleeding for almost two weeks, and sometimes I spot in between the heavy times."

"Well, not that you want to hear this, but you're peri-menopausal, Chelle. Some women are like this as they get closer to menopause."

"I'm only forty!"

"It's that time. I know you hate to hear it."

"But it happened right after the abortion." She says the last part quietly, as if the nurse shouldn't hear it.

"I can't do an internal with so much bleeding. Can you come back next week?"

Chelle sighs. "Yes, I can."

"Okay. Chelle, have you sought any help for your depression we'd discussed last time?" As he speaks, he uses both hands to push on her abdomen rhythmically. Her insides roil as if they are alive.

"I'm fine. I just had a moment, that's all."

He drops his chin and smiles. "Chelle, come on. Talk to me."

"I—" she stops and the events of the past month coalesce into a single, white-hot memory of Dan's face when she told him she knew. About *her*. "I'm fine." She opens and closes her hand, watching as her fingers curl around each other like an infant's.

Dr. Montaigne listens to her belly, silent as the blink of an eye, while the quiet surrounds her. Chelle looks around, seeing and not seeing the room she had been in before—or was it farther down? The rooms all look the same; they are soothing like a lullaby until there is blood. She steels herself against the barrage of images that accompany the memory.

Mostly the horror of wondering if Marin would come back in the new child, plotting to leave her after only fifteen years, all over again.

She could not bear it.

"Chelle, how are you really?"

"Okay. I'm—I'm fine, really."

"Okay. Have you thought more about a tubal ligation?"

"No. I don't think I want that anymore."

"You're not worried about another accidental pregnancy?"

"No, actually. Hell no. I mean, I really think I'm safe."

Dr. Montaigne walks to the desk and scribbles loudly. He hands her a prescription. "A week, Chelle. Here's a pad if you need it."

"Thanks. I'll see you in a week."

When he exits, she robotically gets dressed. As she leaves she closes the door gently, as if laying a child down to sleep.

She walks out of the office and once outside she almost laughs. Chelle's concern is not for herself. Her concern is that Marilyn will get pregnant and Dan will leave to raise a child with her. Perhaps he'll want two or three children with her. Perhaps four…how many children would he want Marilyn to bear him?

Dan never even knew about Chelle and his child of seven weeks. Chelle still isn't sure if she could ever tell him.

৩৩

Callie's hand remains poised in front of the door as her breathing quickens slightly. Her heartbeat pulses in her throat so that her tongue won't let her swallow. Her hand waits patiently.

She finally raps on the wood, the hollow sound echoing loudly throughout the whole neighborhood. She glances up the street, sure people will teem out of their houses in droves to see the girl who survived. To condemn her.

Callie's feet have minds of their own and they begin to shuffle backwards, back toward the steps and to safety. Just then, the door yawns open, and it takes her a moment to understand who she sees.

Marin's father winces as the sunlight accosts his eyes. He looks as though he's been sleeping.

Callie opens her mouth to speak, but it no sound comes out. Her eyes do all the talking.

Dan searches her face, then looks down. When his gaze returns, his eyes are red and shadowed. "I don't know why, but I almost told you Marin's not here." He lets out a harsh laugh, then shakes his head.

Callie feels her whole body retreat, yet she doesn't move. "Mr. Shaw...I'm here to see your wife..."

"Call me Dan. You're here to see Chelle?"

"Yeah."

Suddenly his eyes turn wary. He licks dry lips and tilts his head. "She isn't here. Can I give her a message?"

"She told me to come by. So I thought ...I would."

Dan gnaws on his inner lip, clearly needing to speak. Callie doesn't want to know what he has to say because she saw them together. She had never even accidentally seen her *father* with her mother—but she'd seen them. She'd hated how she felt—the strange mixture of curiosity and revulsion.

"She told you to come by, huh?"

"Yeah."

"Hm. Well, do you want to come in?"

Callie scowls. He seems less friendly than when she first got here, but now he's inviting her in. She lowers her gaze and then levels it at him.

"Okay."

He stands aside and she steps in cautiously. The back of her neck tickles with the door closing behind her in the familiar room. She looks down and she has gooseflesh all over her bare legs. She wraps her arms around herself and smiles at him as he stands and regards her.

"You grew up, huh?" His smile is pleasant but weary.

She nods. "I guess. Yeah."

"Yeah...um, have a seat. You want something to drink?"

"Sure."

"What would you like?"

"Whatever you've got," she calls after his retreating form. Callie tries to imbue her voice with confidence in the hopes he'll give her some wine or beer. Free booze is always good.

She reaches into her front pocket, tight against her body, and she pulls out a pill, swallowing it convulsively. For a moment she wonders if she'll choke. She could die right there and the irony of that chills her even more. She wonders what he would do. Would he let her die?

Dan walks back into the room with a beer in one hand and her heart jumps. Then she sees her iced tea.

"Beer's better," she says, pouting a little.

He smiles a half smile and sits opposite her. Her glass sits innocuously on the table in front of her. She watches the ice shift inside the glass as the pill works its way into her. Callie leans back and crosses her long legs and suddenly she can breathe just fine.

"So what can we do for you? It's been a long time."

"It has, yeah." Callie remembers the way his hands covered her mother's body, how violent it seemed. Her breathing speeds up and soon it isn't her mother he's fucking, but some woman and she watches and becomes fascinated with her private show.

"How're things? You in school?"

"Yeah, the community college for now."

"Hey, nothing wrong with that." His eyes flick to her legs and he blinks rapidly. She uncrosses her legs and crosses them again. Her shorts are very short. Callie instinctively knows how to play it. *She always has.*

"So do you still work at UPS?" She speaks to him like an adult. *She* is an adult. She wishes her mother could watch his face.

"Yep. Still doin' the time. How's your mom and dad?"

She lowers her face but keeps her gaze on his eyes. She had only been with one older man, a man older than her father. He was her economics professor last semester. He's married, too. She licks her lower lip and smiles. "They're great, actually. Never been better, really." Her smile brightens as she watches his eyes darken.

"That's great. Well, Chelle doesn't get home 'til about six. If you wanna come back..."

"Okay. Maybe I will." She stands, unbending her legs first while her body is slow to rise. She languidly straightens, extending her arms above her head and sighing as she releases the stretch. "Thanks, Dan. For the tea."

"Sure thing." He does that rapid eye blink again and she knows she got to him. And if she got to him, she got to her mother, too.

൭

"Jesus Christ." Dan is still shaking. The girl came out of nowhere, standing on the stoop, and his heart breaks because with her standing there, it's as if he had Marin back, if only for a few moments. The moments when he hoped she might be just upstairs.

And Callie's changed. She has her mother's long limbs, but she isn't as thin. Her legs are muscular and tan and seemed to take over his vision when she'd sat down. Dan reaches down between his legs and his partially stiff dick quivers when he thinks of the small indent he glimpsed as she opened her legs to cross them; opened her legs to stand.

He grew up in the Seventies, where camel toe crotches, short-shorts and Farrah Fawcett hair gave him his masturbation fodder every night. Five minutes ago, he had every one of those triggers on his couch. He fights for control as he stares at where she sat.

He tells himself she's his lover's daughter. He tells himself she was his daughter's best friend and he forces himself to see Marin as a young woman, but that results in the unwanted visual of his wife's face and full breasts and crotch indents, seams slipping in between legs and into moist, warm places where his hands like to travel.

He grabs his phone and searches for Marilyn's number, as if she is a talisman against his evil thoughts, thoughts about her daughter and his own daughter, Marin, who's now amalgamated with his wife forever.

He stares at Marilyn's number and her face on his phone and his hand can't move to call her. He moves the contact list down to Chelle's number, knowing she will come home tired, angry, spent.

Chelle would not allow him in her bed, probably ever again. She knows about Marilyn now and stubbornly refuses to talk about it. He wants to hash it out with her; get permission, get vilified, get something other than the same silence he'd gotten when Marin died, the stoic presence of a rigid ghost. Even though she knows about Marilyn, it occurs to him suddenly that Chelle has never once asked him to stop.

No, he doesn't dial Marilyn. She hasn't returned his calls since the night at The Center. Chelle is gone. He allows his mind to wander to the couch and watches the place where Callie had been. He eases his sweats down.

9

The corners of Marilyn's mouth spasm. She is taut, a string being pulled by the urge to laugh, the urge to wail. The paper has been folded into sixths, and won't stay closed. It had made an interesting crease in Cliff's pants. She pulls on it to flatten so she can read.

The hotel had been for one day.

The thought of Cliff having an affair has never occurred to her. She has always taken his devotion for granted. Cliff sharing his body with someone else doesn't matter so much as sharing his loyalty. She isn't sure she can live with that.

She smoothes out the receipt on the dresser and it stays stubbornly creased, the paper elevated up by the folds. She almost caresses it flat, coaxing it to obey her. The brutal truth is that she had shared it all with Dan: heart, mind, body...*loyalty*. It's what makes this moment so exquisitely painful. She smells the page and it smells of Cliff's cologne.

Cliff doesn't know about Dan, she's sure. He'd suspected others, but never knew them, and so she can play the part, the crying, wailing, the *how could you do this to me—to us?* She could wave the evidence in his face, creases and all. But she won't.

She folds the receipt against each fold, until it's level, lying on the dresser, a flat page. And that's where she plans to keep it.

The creases still remain, but she can see the writing on the receipt as clear as day. Her breath quickens.

A moment of rage overtakes her and she grasps the receipt and encloses the page entirely in her hand, squeezing until creases and folds are all that remain of it.

༄

Silence is a wife's prerogative. Silence is the only weapon a wife has when she knows. Chelle refuses to reward him with her thoughts, her feelings, her pain. He has not earned it. Instead, he's earned silence.

She flips on the light and Dan's face is bleary with sleep. "Oh..."

"Why are you in my bed?" Chelle tosses her purse on the chair near the door.

"I was...I was napping and fell asleep."

Chelle stares at him. "'You were napping and fell asleep?'"

Dan smiles, "Yeah. Can you come here?"

"No, I'm physically incapable of going there."

Dan stares at her and her anger, her hurt, and her humiliation spread through her chest like wildfire in dry desert. He looks like an innocent little boy with his hair standing up on end, sleep gracing puffy eyes. She hates that she feels tenderness toward him.

"Please?"

"What do you want, Dan?"

"Well, for you to come here, that's a start."

"Are you still seeing her?"

Dan stares at her, the smile fading from his face. "Not really."

"What does that mean, 'not really'? You either are or you aren't."

"It's...I'm...I love you, Chelle."

"That is the most insulting thing you could say to me right now. It's like a parent spanking his kid while telling him it hurts him more than it hurts the kid. You're a hypocrite."

"Okay...you wanna share feelings? Good. Let's start sharing our feelings. Let's start with this: I want to talk to you about Marin. Our daughter. Remember her?"

Chelle huffs a breath out and strides to the bed. "Don't you turn this around on me! You have no right to talk about her, you asshole! You dare mention her in the same breath with your fucking-whore mistress?"

Dan's face loses light, as if a switch is thrown, as if she has no right to insult the woman he sleeps with. Chelle wraps her arms in front of her chest, wound up tight like a spool of twine.

He opens his mouth and she's waited for that. "Get out of my bed, and out of my house. I want you to *leave*, Dan!"

His nostrils flare for a brief moment and he bows his head, as if he ponders the imperative like it's a request. He nods because it's the only thing he can do. He moves to the other side of the bed, pivots to place his feet on the floor and stand. Smoothing his hair back, he wanders from the room as if in a trance.

Chelle slams the door behind him and stumbles over to the bed. She's angry at herself; she allowed him to see a small piece of her pain. Lying on the bed, she covers her face with her hands. She broke her silence and now she unravels.

෮

Cliff stares at his wife, waiting for her to acknowledge him. She's reading the newspaper and she never reads the newspaper.

"I *asked* where Callie was, Marilyn."

"Gone." She shrugs. The teapot's whistle unnerves him as its quiet whistle begins to crescendo. Marilyn stands, her eyes empty, and pulls the pot off of the burner.

"I thought we could all go out to dinner tonight. As a family." *A family unit.*

"Did you?" Marilyn's vacant stare has him wondering if she's taking the anti-anxiety pills again. He watches her staccato movements as she pulls a cup from the cupboard.

She pours water and doesn't drop in a tea bag. The water's steam just rises impotently and his face feels as though the steam drenches it.

"Why don't you have your tea and I'll go get changed."

Cliff would have normally kissed her cheek, but it seems to be gone, her cheek. It's sunken into her face and all that's left is a skeletal cheekbone, harsh, near her eyes where she can see everything.

He plods up the stairs, his eyes on Callie's bedroom door. He can feel its emptiness from where he is. He won't even knock. If she'd been home, her music would be on. There would be life on the other side, emanating under the door and reassuring him. Whenever she's not home, he panics a little.

Their sunny bedroom has so many windows he wonders how they get any privacy at all.

The slippery sound of his tie sliding from his shirt pleases him. He unbuttons each button, the starched lapels rough against his fingers. His stiff shirt almost crackles as he pulls it off. The dresser is clean, no dust. Marilyn cleaned today. As he places his tie on the dresser top, he looks down then at the garbage can.

There is one piece of paper in it, crumpled into a tight ball. He reaches in for it and unravels the mess, heart in his throat. It's the hotel receipt from his rendezvous with Chelle.

There's no personality to how the paper had been crumpled. He can't tell if he'd crumpled it and tossed it away earlier, or it had been tossed for him. A sour taste in his mouth causes him to clear his throat. He glances into the mirror, and his face is skeletal, too. There's no blood in it, no life. There is only the blank stare of someone in the throes of a quiet panic.

❦

Callie's face hurts from smiling. Her arm hurts from holding up her phone.

The flash goes off and she and Ryanne accidentally bump heads together again.

They lie on their backs next to each other and Ryanne holds up her phone next.

"Okay, do a total drama face." They both scowl and Ryanne's flash goes off.

"What are you doing?" Callie watches her.

"Putting it on Facebook."

"Oh God, don't do that, my *mother* looks at that."

"You friended your *mother?*"

"No! She friended....me." Ryanne's laugh echoes inside the small room. They had smoked and fell asleep inside the warehouse that afternoon. It's now seven o'clock in the evening.

"Who keeps texting you?" Ryanne props herself up on one elbow and looks down at Callie.

"My parents."

"Uh oh, you gonna be in trouble?"

Callie smiles up at her. "No."

Silence engulfs them as Callie pulls her eyes toward Ryanne's intense gaze. As her smile fades, Ryanne moves closer, leaning down toward Callie's parted lips. Callie's breathing quickens and the sounds in the warehouse become frighteningly loud. More people have arrived. She wants to look at the door, see if anyone approaches. But all she sees is Ryanne's approach.

For a brief moment Callie's forgotten how to kiss as Ryanne's lips melt onto hers. It'd been so long since she'd kissed a girl. Maybe one other after Marin. The kiss is the softest fur being rubbed throughout her whole being. She rolls toward Ryanne slightly and touches her face. When Ryanne's hand cups her breast, her touch is tender and yet firm, so unlike a guy's groping, rough hands. And that's when Callie pushes her away.

"Wait!" Callie's eyes are open wide, her forehead creased.

"What?"

"I just...wanna wait."

Ryanne tilts her head to the side. "That's chill. I didn't expect anything or...anything."

"Well you seemed to."

"I'm not some asshole guy who brought you here to fuck." Ryanne's face is cold, her stare hostile. "I wouldn't have done anything you didn't want me to."

"What makes you think I even wanted *that?*" Callie covers her chest and knows she lies. Her heart pounds and the blood pulses through her like a rabid tide. She drowns in her own breath. *Liar.*

"Well you sure as hell seemed to want it. What the hell's wrong with you? You give off these 'come fuck me' signals and when I kiss you, you're fine, then when you start feeling something, you call it off."

"I didn't feel anything." Callie sits up, suddenly cold.

"Bullshit." Ryanne moves closer to her and gets near her ear. "Bullshit you didn't." Ryanne's face is open, her eyes tender.

Callie lays her forehead on her bent knees. "I just want to go."

The only visual Callie has is Ryanne's boots. They don't move and she's all at once panicked and afraid that they will, leaving her to herself. She desperately wants to look up and see her, but she can't, she won't.

"Come on, then." Ryanne says, voice sharp. "I'll take you home."

༄

"The ice is thin come on dive in,
underneath my lucid skin
the cold is lost, forgotten…
Tied down to this bed of shame,
Tried to move around the pain but oh,
your soul is anchored…"
~Sara McLaughlin

PART II

November, 2006

1
_____

S he couldn't stop the small yelp of excitement from escaping her.

She had gained five—no, *six pounds*.

That would put her at 109 lbs. Cliff would be so happy.

Callie? Callie would smile and tell her 'that's great, Mom', but Marilyn knew Callie and knew that fifteen-year-olds don't understand anything about why mothers get sick; they only resent the fact that they are not impervious to it.

She pulls her light pink sweat suit from the hanger and holds it in front of her. Does she dare try clothes without draw strings?

They hadn't taken everything. One ovary remains. Her uterus remains. She went against her doctor's advice and only removed the offending organ, not taking the full step to a hysterectomy. And she's glad. Maybe some-day...could she even carry another child?

Laying the sweats aside, she grabs her jeans off of the shelf, the top pair, dark and rich, the ones with large stitching. The legs fit and she shimmies the other leg on her. When she pulls them up, the waistband stands out and away from her belly and its sagging flesh, giving her a clear view of her panties. She presses them against her but they are stubborn and pooch back out.

She pulls them down, the fabric almost abrading her thin skin. Her skin still hurts. She is brittle everywhere.

Marilyn rubs her hand over her belly, the skin sagging slightly from the rapid weight loss brought on by the illness and then the chemo. She doesn't feel she has ownership of her own flesh anymore. It had been invaded. She doesn't dare to press harder.

The jeans crackle as she folds them and grabs an older, softer pair. They are faded and comfortable. After just one leg in, she can tell the thighs will drown her. Had she ever been this big?

She places her hand carefully over where they had removed her ovary and the ache there is still ever-present—a reminder. She stares in the mirror at her emaciated frame and vows to get breast implants. She looks deflated in every part of her that ought to be cushioned and soft. Her eyes are huge.

She feels down her shelf for the next pair of jeans. She chooses a pair that is skinny and has spandex. She should be able to wear them. She pulls them on—they actually hug her legs! But the rear view is discouraging. The material under her ass puckers slightly.

Her doctor's words haunt her.

Seventeen percent.

That's the survival rate for her "particular brand of nasty."

Marilyn shudders. She pulls the pants up and searches for a belt. The total hysterectomy would have been brutal upon the brutality of the treatments. Had she taken the coward's way out? Had she doomed herself to a repeat performance of this nightmare?

The belt doesn't help. It causes her to look like a child wearing her older sister's hand-me-down's. She yanks them down and leaves them and the rest of the jeans on the floor.

The sweat pants are cool against her slightly sore legs. Callie would just have to deal with her coming to get her in yet another sweat suit.

But at least the scarves are a thing of the past. Callie had hated those. She said they made Marilyn look sick.

∽

When Dan and Marin Shaw come home, they smell bacon.

Chelle stands at the stove smoking a cigarette and the sizzling crowds out the noise of the door opening.

"Hey, Honey."

Chelle turns and her gaze falls immediately on Marin. "Oh my God, you didn't wear *that* to church, did you?"

"At least she goes to church, dear."

Marin is silent, eyes on her phone. Dan places his arm around his daughter.

"Ya know, Marin, even God takes a day off from texting."

"Funny, Daddy."

"You went way over your text limit last month, Marin. You need to stop talking to Callie so much. We have a home phone, for that, you know?" Chelle flips a pancake, the smoke off of the griddle clouding the light in the kitchen.

"You don't know it's Callie."

Chelle's face becomes hard. "Do I look stupid to you?"

"No, you don't look *stupid*." Marin's posture tells Chelle something different.

"Good, because I know the goddamned number by heart from the cell phone bill!"

"*Okay*!"

Dan steps in between them and hugs Chelle, "It's fine, Honey—"

"Oh, it's fine for you, you don't pay the cell bill. And look at her attitude toward me!"

"Honey," Dan moves to kiss her cheek. Chelle shrugs him off and places bacon, still sizzling, on a plate of paper towels. The pancakes are expertly flipped and the smell reminds Dan of home, but the air is chilly, the air conditioner on full blast.

Marin sits on a chair, crosses her legs and continues to text.

"Take off that dress, Marin; you look like a slut." Chelle takes another drag off her cigarette as Marin stares at her father, then Chelle. Tears well up in Marin's eyes and her chair knocks back into the table as she bolts from the room.

"Jesus, why did you tell her that?"

"Because she does. No wonder that guy broke up with her. She dresses like a whore."

"Chelle, don't talk about her like that!"

Her eyes are dangerous and she regards him. "I would think you would be more protective of your own daughter! I know how men think!"

"I am protective, but there's more ways than one to tell her to dress properly."

"Oh? Like telling her she looks nice every time she comes out of her room?"

"I don't—"

"You do! Do you want to be grandparents in our thirties?"

"No, I can safely say that thought doesn't appeal to me."

"Okay, then." The matter is closed for Chelle, and she turns back to the hot cakes on the griddle, now dark brown. They are burning, the middle is raw. She turns down the heat but it's too late.

Chelle hears Dan's laughter from behind her and she turns around to see her daughter descend the stairs.

She's wearing several pairs of sweats, shirts, and a coat. Her head is wrapped in a scarf—burka style. Marin's eyes are not friendly. "How's this, Mom. Oh, shit, my feet are showing."

Dan's chuckling infuriates Chelle and she hurls the spatula at Marin. It bounces off the wall next to her and onto the floor. The laughter stops.

Chelle whirls on Dan. "*You* encourage her disrespect. And you—get upstairs and get busy on homework! You're grounded for the week, smart ass. How's that for funny?" Chelle's face is dark stone and she walks toward Marin and snaps the spatula off the floor. "Last time I make you idiots breakfast."

Chelle stalks back to the griddle, scoops up every pancake and tosses them in the trash. Dan stares at her quietly, eyes sad, and finally he stands and walks up the stairs, hand on Marin's shoulder.

Chelle stares at the cakes in the garbage and her brow creases as her eyes close tight.

It's always busy on Fridays at the grocery store because of the International Wine specials.

Cliff picks up a bottle from New Zealand because he thinks Marilyn will want to try wine tonight. The nausea has faded. She's getting better, and with that, a new breath of life has invaded them both.

Mangoes are lined up like rows of supple breasts and he passes his hand over them, caressing them. The smell causes him to daydream about tropical fruits, places with umbrellas in sand and beverages, and heat diminished only by the sea-surf breeze. Marilyn and he could be together and she'd be all his—for a good long while, and that's all he's ever asked of Marilyn. It's all he's ever been able to ask.

He picks up the mango and inhales, smelling only cardboard and a sickly mixture of cloying sweetness. He squeezes the fruit and when it gives to the slight pressure, he places it in a bag.

It isn't that he's fooled. He knows. She's even admitted it to him in those heavy moments of drunken passion, when he's pounded it out of her between thrusts, and her confessions had caused him to rupture mercilessly inside her. Those moments bound her to him, invisible strings tying her sins with his munificence and compassion, his aching lust. He understands her need. He sees it in her with every new lover.

But what she doesn't understand is his need. The others only fuel it, and the thoughts of it stir him almost immediately so that he steps closer to the cart. His need, coupled with a deep thrumming of hurt creates a familiar dissonance in him that arouses him profoundly.

Every cloud has a silver lining. And his silver lining is that he gets to have her. All of her. None of the others can or would ever be able to say that. They are distractions. Yet they serve his needs, too.

Of course she had loved a few. But Marilyn was not a fool. She knew where she would get the most freedom. She knew which side of her bread was buttered—and not in terms of money, either. She hungers to be needed, and he needs her, aches for her. The illness had sanitized their marriage bed, but now she's coming back to life and so is he.

He places his hand around a large coconut and has an urge to break it open then and there, to see the moist center of it, to smell its scent, bury his face in its flesh.

He looks up and just by chance his neighbor, Mrs. Barrow, catches his eye. He smiles and nods but it will not be enough. She'll come to him, and she does. He moves closer to the cart.

"Hello, Dr. Erickson. How's Marilyn feeling these days?"

The elderly woman's gaze is glassy and pink lines her eyes. He smiles and replaces the coconut.

"She's feeling great. In two weeks it's her six-week follow up. We're quite optimistic."

"Oh good, good. She looked absolutely ravishing the other night."

"I'm sorry?"

"At that little Italian place Ken and I go to on Thursdays. It's veal night on Thu—"

"That wasn't Marilyn."

"Oh, I'm sure it was. You weren't with her?"

"No. She was home resting that night."

His cock is full, ripe, needing to be pressed against flesh. The sensation is delicious as he stares off, just behind Mrs. Barrow's ear.

"Oh, excuse me. I'm so embarrassed. I thought surely...well, good luck to you and tell Marilyn to take care now."

Mrs. Barrow's task is complete. She'd come to inform him. He'd known it on some level. And it's alright that he knows. His breath comes faster. What isn't alright is when Mrs. Barrow knows. She will walk to every house and tell them about how she'd seen Marilyn with someone else and how could she do that to poor Dr. Erickson after he'd stayed by her side during her cancer....

Only he can know about his wife. His protective nature is in shards as he thinks of Marilyn and, at the same time, his growing erection. Where *had* he been Thursday? Ah, the symposium at the hospital. Marilyn said she had been home all night. She'd casually mentioned re-connecting with an old friend over email. Garn is his name. She always told half-truths to make it fine.

The fruits' smells no longer appeals to him. They suddenly seem bruised and over-ripe. Without taking them from the bag, he places them on top of the group of mangos, disturbing their pristine formation. They blur in front of him.

His vision becomes focused as he wonders if he has ever met Garn; then it doesn't matter. A checkout line opens and he strides to it with the two bottles of wine, one in front of his pants. All he can think about now is taking his wife.

2

Callie gazes at the ceiling in the small room and watches it move back and forth as if she's on a ship. Marin had been curled up against her sleeping for a while, and now she stirs. She'd been inconsolable.

Marin sniffs again, shifting, and Callie hugs her closer. Marin's grief soothes Callie's aching insides, the serpent that coils within her in the dark.

The small blue pills she takes from her mother don't hold the same magical properties they once did. All they do now is make the ceiling move.

The boy is eighteen. Marin said he'd made her 'a woman'. He said he was Marin's boyfriend. Then she saw him last night while out with her parents and he'd been with a tall blond girl, a cheerleader at their high school. When he saw Marin, he'd laughed.

Marin says she's going to hell. She is going to hell because good girls didn't lose their virginity at fifteen and good girls don't get pregnant and Marin is five days late. Good Catholic girls never carry protection. They don't need it.

Callie has lived through every new physical and sexual line crossed by Marin. Every step, every move, toward Marin's deflowering—Callie was there. Callie had superimposed herself on the boy, and so it was *her* mouth that kissed Marin's, her hands that felt Marin's breasts, her fingers that touched her *there*.

The serpent remains inside. It coils around Callie's vital organs, and she even pictures its black coils intertwining with her guts, her innards. When she cries, she can feel a part of it come up her throat and then she vomits, expecting black scales to issue from her.

And she angers it. When she cries she angers it and the pain is worse after, as if it injects poison into every muscle, every fiber. So she tries to bury her tears so they never gurgle past her throat.

Callie shifts so that her face is in Marin's hair. Coconut and florals infuse the soft curls and Callie opens her mouth to kiss them, inhaling the scent of her, wanting to pull her closer until Marin invades her, quashing the black thing that plagues Callie's guts. The only time it subsides is when Callie's with Marin, when Callie holds Marin.

Callie stops thinking and her hand strays down to Marin's breast. She cups it gently and kisses Marin's hair. As she caresses her, she feels Marin's head move. When she opens her eyes, they are met by Marin's gaze. Callie doesn't move her hand. She can't. She only has breath that stays in her lungs and expands with fear. Marin doesn't move her hand either. They stay like that, and Marin's eyes close and she moves her arm up to press Callie's hand onto her breast firmly.

Callie releases her held breath, and kisses Marin's hair again. They lie there, intertwined, and the ceiling moves and the serpent, it sleeps.

❧

"You bring me *vino?*"

"No, Mama, you know you can't drink here."

"Eh. That's the bad thing about getting old. People don't treat you like people no more."

"You're on so many medications, you'd get sick if I brought you wine, Mama."

"Mija, you bring it and drink it and I'll make a toast to you."

"I'm in recovery, Mama. You know that." Chelle places her hand on her mother's limp wrist and rubs her back as she coughs. The watery noise rattles painfully in Chelle's ears.

The old woman's lined face twists in a grimace. She shifts and pulls her hospital gown around her thin frame. Her dark eyes are gigantic against her gaunt face. "Eh. Gods, you can't be no sissy, MiChelle. It takes some *cojones* to get old."

"So you tell me. Here, have another sip of water."

The old woman waves it away and stares past her daughter. "They come for me. The angels come for me, Chelle. I can feel them. What do you mean you're in recovery? What does that mean?"

"You know, Mama."

"What do you mean?"

"Mama, I can't drink anymore. I'm an alcoholic. I always drink too much then I hurt myself, you understand?" She doesn't remind her of how she hurts others, too. So many others.

"Eh, could be like your papa. He hurt me, though."

"I know he did, Mama."

The old woman's eyes redden and she cries, sniffling and moaning quietly.

"Shh, it's alright now, you're alright."

"Did he hurt you, Mija? Did he ever—"

"No, Mama. No, he never hurt Peter or me."

"I made sure it was always me..."

"I know you did. Shh, let's talk about something else."

But the old woman continues to cry. "I can hear his voice even now...'Manuela, come here! What have you done?' *His eyes were the devil's eyes when he drank, Mija.*"

"I know, and I don't drink anymore because my eyes get that way too."

She looks over to her daughter and smiles. "You just have to stop, Chelle. You understand?"

"Yes, I know. Why don't you rest? *Por favor, el resto.* Okay? I'll come back tomorrow."

"Eh, that's a good girl. You know that's good. I don't know why he was so angry. I never know why he get so angry."

"Shh. It's alright, Mama."

The old woman's cough racks her and the drowning continues as she gasps for air.

Chelle walks over to the door and opens it, snapping her head back and forth, looking down the hall.

A nurse rounds the corner and Chelle thrusts her hand out of the door, waving for her. "Excuse me? My mother—she's...I'm wondering if there's anything you can do for her pain?"

"Let's see what we can do." The nurse plucks the old woman's chart from the wall and studies it. Chelle opens the door wide and the nurse strides in, eyes on her patient. Her voice reverberates along the wall as she speaks much louder than she needs to. "Are you in pain, Manuela?"

The old woman opens her eyes and smiles. "Eh, not so bad. Have you met my favorite niece? This is Chelle..."

"I'm your daughter, Mama." Chelle's voice squeezes through the tight opening of her throat and her mother smiles.

"She's a good girl. She don't drink like her...ooh!" Her crying begins anew and the nurse looks apologetically at Chelle.

"I'll check her chart and see what we can give her."

"I'm her daughter."

The nurse smiles and it's tinged with sadness as she leaves. Chelle watches her mother study the space at her bedside, eyes teary as she speaks to the angels there.

৩৩

A brief knock and Marilyn walks in.

Callie is in front of the mirror and she jumps back, startled.

"Mom!"

Marilyn has Callie's laundry basket, her arms aching from the weight of it. "You left these in the dryer and I have laundry to do—honey, what are you wearing?"

Callie walks over and grabs a pair of jeans. "I'm wearing underwear. Jeez, you should knock—"

"That isn't 'underwear', that's lingerie!"

The girl rolls her eyes and Marilyn drops the basket. It tips over. Marilyn stoops to right the basket, watching Callie get dressed.

"It just matches, that's all—"

"When did you get those?"

"We went shopping Saturday, remember?"

"You and Marin."

"Yes...you *do* remember, right?"

Marilyn grabs the clothes from the basket that had spilled to the floor and shoves them firmly into the pile, her heart racing. "Why in the hell do you need lingerie? Who's going to see you?"

"*No one*, jeez."

"Then why have it?" Marilyn straightens up, the remainder of the clothes piled around the front of the basket. "I'll let you pick these up."

"Everybody wears thongs—"

"Oh, yeah, like strippers! And that isn't a thong, that's a g-string."

"Same diff."

"See, this is why I told you that I don't trust Marin. Every time you hang out with her, you push the boundaries—"

"Of underwear?"

"You know exactly what I mean. She dresses way too old for a fifteen-year-old. She dates that boy, that—"

"They broke up, and anyway, I'm going to be sixteen in the Spring. You can't keep me a child forever!"

Marilyn stares at the stranger who has taken over her little girl. She has full lips, golden blond hair, and tanned skin from hours at the pool. A mother's walking nightmare. Marilyn's head nods forward a little. "I'm going to go lie down. I'm tired. No more of that—that *crap,* Callie. You can wear normal underwear."

"Oh my God, like it even matters!"

"It matters to me."

"Marin's mom—"

"Oh, don't even get me *started* on that! If her mother cared, she'd make her daughter put some damn clothes on!"

"This is about you hating my best friend! This isn't about my fucking panties!"

"*You watch your mouth!*"

"You hate her!"

"I never said that."

"You don't like her."

"I worry—"

"Don't worry. She cares about me and I care about her, okay?"

Marilyn stares at her daughter's quivering lip and wonders when the care she has for her daughter became less important.

Callie's mirror holds pictures of her and Marin, making faces, smiling, pouting. Marilyn's stomach twists into angry knots. "Get your laundry done."

Callie stares at her with an open mouth as she closes the bedroom door and steps back into the hall.

In the hall Marilyn's laundry sits in a basket, only it's twice the size of Callie's basket. She stoops down and lifts it with a grimace. In her bedroom, she drops it unceremoniously onto the floor; it topples and rolls onto its side, dumping its contents.

"Perfect."

The clothes remain on the floor as she stares at her thong underwear that had toppled onto the carpet.

3 _____

Dan had never seen Marin so restless. Two years ago she had been a shining example of selflessness and charity when he brought her to Sacred Heart. Now she is withdrawn and sullen. He knows it's her age. Her age and her choices. He readies himself.

"Mar, come here a sec."

She doesn't respond to him. She merely pulls her feet off of the desk with a 'thunk' and sits up in her chair.

"Did I stutter? Come here." Dan smiles to take the edge off, but his irritation shows on his face. "I think it's time you learn what it is we do here." He swallows heavily and wipes the forming band of sweat from his forehead.

"I know what we do here, Daddy. We tell pregnant girls to have their babies."

"No. That isn't all we do. We change lives, save lives, here. If we make something like an abortion real for people, it changes their outlook forever, do you understand that?"

For one brief moment her eyes flood with rage. He gazes at this young woman who, until recently, shared everything with him. He wants to enclose her in his arms and tell her it will all be alright. He tries a different tact.

"Marin, how would you feel about changing schools?"

"What? Why!"

"Relax, it was just a question. I thought going to St. Catherine's—"

"Are you *kidding* me?"

"You were all for it last year—"

"No, I was all for it when I was twelve, Dad. I'm not going!"

"Fine. I just want to have a conversation. Remember? Those things you and I used to have on occasion that involved *both* of us—*talking?*"

Marin rolls her eyes. Dan regards his daughter, clearly struggling, clearly unhappy. He remembers feeling angst every day of his adolescence, but by her age, he'd lost his mother and younger brother. He'd learned early on how mortality interconnected them all.

"Mar, talk to me."

"Okay, I don't wanna be here. I wanna go home and call my friends and do my homework and be...normal!" Tears form in her eyes and she quickly wipes them away.

"'Normal' meaning thinking only of yourself, Marin. That's not a good way to live your life."

"I don't know if I believe in this—this—"

"This what?" Dan's mind swims and he walks over to her, brow furrowed. "C'mon, I wanna show you something. Something I think you need to see."

Marin sullenly stands and he places his hand on her back, gently leading her toward the hallway. As they approach the darkened room, she stops, recoiling.

"I don't want to."

"Marin, if you don't believe in what we do here, you need to start believing."

"So you're going to make me watch some gross movie showing a baby getting sucked out? Dad, this is *so* wrong."

"It *is* wrong! Don't you get that?"

"Why are you telling me this!"

"Because I know." His voice cracks. The perspiration tickles his face as it slides down past his ear. It begins to cool, but he knows his anguish shows like a marquee. He'd emptied her bathroom garbage.

"Know...what?" Marin is cautious, moving slowly away from him.

"I *know*, Marin. Your mom and I can help. We'll adopt the baby—"

"I don't know what you're talking about!"

"I found the test."

"It wasn't mine!"

"Whose was it?"

"How should I know?" She's openly weeping now. He tries to touch her and she shrinks back.

"Marin, stop. Your mom and I—"

"What did you tell her?"

"Nothing! I thought you—"

"Leave me alone!" She bumps past him and runs down the hall.

It has taken Dan a good half a week to be able to process it, and he knew this might happen. But she'd be back.

He rolls his shoulders back and forth and shakes his head a little to clear the emotion from his face. It will all work out. God's hand is in everything, and soon, he'll have two little girls. He would make it right with God for her and for them.

He breathes rhythmically, calming himself and smiles faintly. The thought of a baby in the house quickens his heart beat and he secretly relishes the idea of the little one blessing his home, revitalizing it. Perhaps Chelle will finally acquiesce to his desire for another child. Or maybe she won't need to.

The baby would have dark hair. It may even be a girl. They could name her after his mother.

෨

Cliff watches his wife for a full five minutes before she sees him. She yelps and opens her eyes wide. "What are you doing?"

"Watching you clean out the closet. You really need to take it easy. You need your rest."

"What good is rest if I don't do anything while I'm rested?" Her wan smile provokes him; he turns around and closes the door to their bedroom.

"Oh, leave it open, I bleached the tub—"

Cliff is down on the floor before she can finish, his lips covering her mouth. She pulls away.

"Cliff, what's wrong with you?"

"I want my wife, is that wrong?" He unfastens his belt and the disinterest in her eyes causes dark thoughts to seep into his mind. There is always a battle between the dark and the heady lust. They feed each other like symbiotic beings, pulling, pushing, invading, retreating. He doesn't wait for her to undress and she makes no move to do so. He pushes her back to the floor, shoes scattering with a sweep of his hand.

"I just sorted those—"

"You're rested up. Re—sort them." He smiles and it's tight, the tumescence in his pants already waning with her frail protests. He grabs her wrist and smells it. "Perfume?"

She yanks it out of his grip. "No—I mean, maybe from earlier—"

"Like when you go out." The blood pulses between his legs now and soon he's turgid and warm again.

Her eyes search his and she seems fragile, caught in her lies, all of them, even the ones from when they were first married. The feeling he gets from it is delicious; the way she acknowledges his power and right and all of those politically incorrect things he embodies. In his throat, he keeps a growl at bay.

Her eyes move to the side and that's long enough for him to free himself and yank down her sweatpants. His hand thrusts between her legs and the heat between them incites him. She's wet and he knows why she's wet now and the dark thoughts fight for presence. He deliberately pictures her in his favorite black dress, perfume dabbed on her wrists for some...*him*, body wash scrubbed on and around her cunt for *him*. Smiling and demurely bowing her head. For *him*. Whoever he is. Maybe that guy—Garn.

Marilyn gasps as he enters her with a look close to helplessness on her face. It's all a part of the game, the dominating of her will, letting her know who's in charge with each slapping thrust violently pushed into her.

"Tell me who you want to fuck." His voice is hoarse through his breath and a small moan escapes her. Marilyn can't ever answer. He goads himself on while she lies perfectly still.

"Would you fuck him and then let me fuck you?"

Her eyes speak volumes to him and he can't understand any of it and it doesn't matter now because whoever was in her will be obliterated by Cliff's manhood, his cock, his *right* to her.

His mouth moves close to her ear. "Garn...it's Garn...is his cock big and fat?"

Her eyes show too much white and with her expression he knows he's right. Knowing the guy's name makes him more real and all of it synchs up in a shuddering blast of light through his vision as he arches over her, moaning, a look of anguish on his face. He's still for a moment, then he collapses, panting.

"I love you." He says it in her ear and ignores the tear sliding past it. She had to know he would find out. She had to know he'd want her.

The thought that she no longer wants him never occurs to him—until now. Before, it had been their game; they had fucked them all together, in a strange way. He got to experience it through her. Now, he fucks no one, and she fucks Garn.

෭

The concoction tastes horrible. Worse than cough syrup mixed with laundry detergent. Callie coughs as she swallows.

"Oh, my God, that's nasty."

Marin giggles and gulps, making a face. "So what is it again? Amaretto—"

"—Sprite and cranberry juice. Shh, don't say 'amaretto' so loud."

"Your Dad's, like, down in the basement and your Mom's, what? Out—"

"Some meeting." Callie shrugs and takes another drink. She scoots closer to Marin. "We should play Truth or Dare."

"What are you, like ten?"

"Shut up!"

"Okay, Truth or Dare."

Callie smiles and rolls her eyes to the ceiling. "Truth."

"Chicken."

"*Truth*."

"Fine. Do you ever you know, like make yourself, like...do you...*you know*."

"*What?*" Callie has a devious smile on her face.

"Touch yourself?" Marin whispers.

Callie grins and rolls onto her back. "Yeah. *All* the time! 'Kay, your turn."

"You are so bad. Okay, *Dare*."

Marin smiles because she's the brave one and Callie is harmless and wouldn't make her do something too horrible. She lies back next to her and watches the ceiling. The small light in the attic room doubles and blurs, moving on the ceiling, then becomes whole again.

"Okay, umm, I dare you to take off your shirt!" Callie laughs and Marin, without hesitation, sits up and pulls the t-shirt she's wearing over her head. She's braless and Callie immediately buckles in laughter, blushing. "Oh my God!"

"Your turn." Marin beams, a drunken glow on her cheeks.

Callie's hand is over her mouth. Then she moves it, jutting her chin out. "Dare. Okay? *Dare*."

Marin smile is wide. "Okay, I dare you to...I dare you to touch them."

Callie snickers and shrugs, showing bravado. "Easy." She reaches over and places her open hand over Marin's exposed breast. She squeezes playfully. Marin winces and recoils.

"Oh, did I hurt you? I just barely—"

"It's fine!" Marin pulls her shirt to her and slips it on.

"I didn't mean to—"

"It's okay, they just hurt really bad."

Callie takes another drink. "Maybe you *are* pregnant." She shudders. "That would suck so bad—"

"I am."

Callie stops and stares, her mouth agape. "Are you fucking kidding me? Why—how come you didn't tell me? And you're drinking!"

"'Cause I wanna lose it, stupid."

"You won't lose it by drinking, you'll just make it all retarded."

"Fuck it. I don't care. I'll do something."

"Can't you—I mean have you told—"

"Of course not! Jesus, can you imagine what my Mom and Dad would say?" Marin thinks of her father's face, the way he's quiet around her now. The way he treats her as if she's a ghost.

"Well, you can't be stupid or you'll hurt yourself, too."

"How do you know, Callie? You don't know shit."

Callie is silent. She leans over to hug Marin and her hand brushes Marin's breast.

"Sorry."

"You are *not*." Marin shudders as if suddenly cold. "You always touch me. Are you a lesbian or what? I mean, it's weird."

"You let me." Callie's eyes are wounded. Marin wants them to be.

"You just do that shit and it's like you *want me* or something."

Callie moves away and bends her knees up, draping her arms across them. She stares at the poster on the far wall. "That's stupid."

They sit silent and still and Marin's head throbs. She glances over to Callie, who looks miserable. Marin bites her lip and scoots closer to her, touching her arm.

"Hey, I'm sorry, okay? I'm just really freaked out. You have to promise you won't tell anyone. Ever."

"I won't tell anyone, ever."

"E—ver."

"I said *okay*! Ever!"

"Okay." Marin pulls Callie toward her and her eyes close, but she's aware of Callie's face, pressed into her hair, inhaling her scent.

෨෧

When Marin laughs, her ample breasts jiggle up and down and Callie tries so hard not to stare.

So many friends lost because Callie never knows how far to go. And all she wants is what other people have and all she wants is to like those strange creatures called boys, but they make her queasy when she thinks of them.

The room tips and it doesn't hurt her head; she flies and closes her eyes. Her stomach flutters because with the warmth of amaretto in her, everything is possible. Having Marin look at her the way she imagines her own gaze graces Marin's face, her body. She is hungry and her hands don't know what to do with themselves when Marin is around because they fidget and become sweaty and hot.

She glances down at Marin's naked hip, exposed by the small t-shirt and low riding sweats and she has the compulsion to run her hands along Marin's creamy coffee skin. She imagines her lips grazing her flesh and with that thought, her heart beats and it threatens to come up her throat. Uncomfortable warmth spreads throughout her lower places and she shifts, sure Marin can smell her, feel her need, and Marin will run.

But now Marin needs her, and the thrill of being needed sings through Callie as her head fills of images of them together, walking hand in hand, never being afraid of discovery. It's the only thing that has brought light to Callie's world and so she holds on to it, desperate to cling to its luminosity, like a flickering torch that keeps evil at bay.

And then Marin tells her about the baby, and she fights to be what she thinks Marin wants and needs. She makes an imprecise vow within her to help Marin in whatever way she needs help. She declares herself to be Marin's protector. But a shift in Marin's eyes and posture makes Callie shy away. She has gone too far. It was an accident, grazing Marin's breast, but she can't be sure because the alcohol makes her clumsy. Marin hisses accusations and she retreats as if stung.

It all comes crashing in around her, the room, the drink, the warmth, the hot places in her mind where she goes to make love to Marin and soon Marin pulls her in, holds her close; she speaks and salves the harsh words. Callie wants to stay away and feel wounded, wants to stay away from the potent hold Marin has over her, but Marin's body melts into her and Callie succumbs to it with a renewed hope that somehow she can save her. She can save her, savor her, and be her savior, and Marin will see the depths of her feeling and never, ever want to let it go.

4

Like coming home. Coming home to soft fragrances and warm fires. But the fire is in her throat and her belly and she pours another shot and downs it in one gulp.

The taste no longer matters and how she dresses it is inconsequential because getting there is home and she hasn't felt at home in so long. So long. But if she's to be completely honest, she has never felt quite like she's all the way home. But she can't stop trying. The small glimpse she gets with every drink is a promise.

Chelle sobs, dry and haggard, and already she reels from the tequila. But more will get her even closer, and so she pours another shot, glad for the reprieve, glad Marin is gone to a sleepover, glad Dan is gone to work, glad her mother is dead. No one to tell her, 'No, no Chelle, you've had too much.' No, *she knows how much* is too damn much and she's not even close.

Her mother died in a hospital bed and Thanksgiving is near, so forever more the holidays will be tainted with pain. Except now the pain won't be from expectations that are unmet and juxtaposed memories of joy and terror. No, now the pain will be of loss and self-inflicted wounds that slowly unravel her mind, until she sleeps without dreams.

Chelle is in the garage, sifting through her boxes, dumping them out. "Where's the goddamned Christmas music?"

Her voice echoes in the empty space and her eyes water as she sings.

"I'm dreaming of a whiiite...Christmas..."

Her sobs come back to her like slashes on her skin and she can't believe how alone she is now. How alone she is when Marin is home and ignores her and rolls her eyes at her with no respect. She shudders because she understands him now. Her father gained respect and she sees it, the wisdom in all of it. She would have never disrespected her father the way Marin does her.

When the garage door opens she screams and places her hand over her chest, swaying on her feet. The car slows and the lights die and she sees Dan's face, all concern, all confusion. She closes her mouth tight, as if her breath will betray her.

He gets out of the car and Chelle decides then and there that if she pretends to be fine she will be fine and so she tells him she wants to hear "White Christmas" because it is her mother's favorite song.

Dan's face enrages her. The expression of sadness so insulting, so insinuating. She wants to slap it off of him and see something else, so she does.

He has her wrist now and she struggles against him and screams for him to just find the goddamned song for her, that's all she needs and the rest is fine.

But he wrestles her inside and doesn't seem to hear that the song is all she needs. He pulls her up to the bedroom and pushes her to the bed and she looks at him with eyes that flame and he watches her, transfixed.

He tells her to lie down and she lifts her shirt for him but he shakes his head, stern and parent-like. She stands and tears at his shirt, pushing at him while tearing the buttons off the stiff, brown uniform. She tells him he's not a fucking man.

When he pushes her back on the bed, the ceiling lamp begins to dance in circles for her and so she watches it dance and sway, and it sways to the music that plays inside her head, over and over. If he could only understand that she just needs that one goddamned song. Then she would be just fine.

She prays to the angels of Christmas, prays they'll help Dan find her mother's song.

He's held his dick in his hand for an hour. Slowly, rhythmically strok-
ing, and then letting his erection wane, he builds up his longing. Marilyn
should have been home an hour ago. Girl's Night Out. They all went to see
some chick flick, but he knows better. The movie lasts ninety minutes. She
has been gone since six. Ah, dinner, he's sure.

Or... Garn fucks her as he sits here with his dick in his hand, the fucking joke of the community while she lets some guy fuck her. His cock
grows harder and he groans. He'd take her over and over, make her never
forget him.

He doesn't even remember the phone call. Callie's friend's father called
to ask if Marin could spend the night there and Cliff remembers feeling
magnanimous for a moment. Of course she could. She's welcome to stay.

He imagines Sunday morning, making breakfast with his wife for the
kids and then watches her in his mind as she shrinks away from him and
he grinds his teeth until his jaw pops. They could make pancakes or waffles
and they would all laugh in the kitchen but Marilyn's eyes don't smile with
him anymore. He tucks his cock back into his pants as he thinks of the
girls, giggling, walking to the kitchen. Noises upstairs alert him and he
adjusts to hide the swelling in his pants.

He takes the last sip of his scotch and the ice clinks with a finality in
the glass as he smacks it onto the table. The basement is cold, the nights
betray the season, and he can't think about all of the up-coming holidays.
They are a stark contrast to the sham his life has become.

He trudges up the stairs and into the main living room and hears nothing more. The kitchen is dark. He mounts the main stairway and listens at
the door to Callie's room. They wouldn't be there, they'd be in the upstairs
attic, Callie's unofficial bedroom, study room, hang out. He's glad he'd had
it finished. He's glad she has somewhere to go and he wishes he did.

He wanders into the hallway and hears the softest sound. A string quartet with a lilting melody that would turn a tide of rats to the sea. The sound
comes from his bedroom and he pushes the door open and hears the water
running. He hadn't heard the garage open, hadn't heard her come in. The
scotch must have dulled his hearing, too. He reaches down and squeezes his
cock, getting it ready for her. Marilyn hadn't been late at all. She'd come

home to him. The shower wasn't for him, though, it was for her. Cliff preferred her smelling like she'd just been fucked.

He rounds the corner slowly and he searches for his wife's lithe, pale frame through the steam. It takes a moment for his eyes to adjust to the small, dark figure in the stall. Cliff closes his eyes tight, then opens them and the blurry image of Marin becomes scathingly clear. Her ample breasts can be seen through the steam, and he sees the dark patch of hair underneath a firm, slightly rounded belly. She turns and her back forms a "c" as it arches into the water. Mesmerized, he stares at her hands as they rub over her flesh and her melody moves in waves over him as a delicious, dizzying pulse plays in his cock.

His hand pushes against the wall, willing him to move, willing him to turn away, yet his feet remain rooted to the floor, the girl no longer a girl, but a vision swept into his life, his home, his shower just for him. He huffs out silently, breathing shallow, and his heart smashes against his ribs. Pain envelopes his face as he grimaces in anguish at his inability to tear his gaze away. Her graceful hands smooth back her long hair and they move over her soapy body and his cock throbs anew with every movement she makes.

As if from a dream, her hand comes up to the glass and wipes away the steam to reveal her dark, astonished eyes, transfixed on his face. She doesn't make a sound. Her mouth opens and her eyes open more and nothing comes because she seems transfixed too, but surely not in the same way. Inside his head he screams out that he's sorry, so sorry. His mouth can't form the words and so he bows his head and trembling, steps away from the wall and rounds the corner into the bedroom.

"Fuck! Jesus…." Cliff mutters and his senses return to him as he moves from the corner where he stands and walks out of the room into the hall. He wants to flee to the basement again. Instead, he leans his back against the wall outside his bedroom. His vision blurs as he imagines her emerging nude, dripping, walking to him, and burying his face in her warm, soft skin. He shakes his head to clear the thought.

But it's too late. The thought arrests him and he clamps his eyes tighter and still the vision plays, sequence by sequence, until he's finally touching her. She's a willing, open vessel to him. Panting, his face slick with sweat, his body shudders as his ears hone in on the shower, still running. The soft string quartet from her lips, however, has grown still. On some level he had to have known. Marilyn doesn't sing.

With much effort, he pushes away from the wall and walks to the top of the stairs. He sees the reflection of his figure in the tall windows over the front door. Wiping his damp face, he descends the stairs, watching all the while toward the driveway for his wife.

⁓

Normal.

Pins and needles tickle her fingertips and head as the amaretto eases its way through her system. She sits quietly while Marin sleeps. Marin's hair is wet from her shower and blankets cover her because after she'd showered she refused to dry off. Her lips are slightly blue. But Marin wants everything to be normal.

Callie's chilled, too, but not from the shower. Her neck has steel bars holding it up. Her shivering is in her legs and her eyes are made of glass, unblinking and transparent. Her hand brushes Marin's hair from her eyes and Callie moves closer to her. By morning, she reassures Marin, things will be normal. But for Callie, 'normal' is wanting to be inside Marin, all the way inside, her head, heart, soul, all of the sappy songs she hears, all of them reminding her how she isn't inside her. Normal.

Marin showered in her parent's shower. It's made of slate. Callie feels like she's in a cave whenever she uses it and she thought it would make Marin feel safe. Callie wants Marin to be safe but she also wants Marin to see past all of that and feel how devoted Callie is to her. She is, after all, helping her get back to normal. She loves Marin enough. Enough to give normal back to her.

The trembling begins to ride up to her stomach and so Callie moves under the blanket with Marin. She tells Marin she's cold, too. Really though, being this close to her vivifies her entire body, and her chest feels like it will implode from the proximity. Her bare legs press against Marin's and she lifts her shirt to press herself alongside her torso. She wants to smell Marin's smell, the coconut and floral-scented hair and candy-flavored perfume she wears, but Marin smells like her mother's shampoo. Callie doesn't care. She still smells like Marin underneath it all.

Callie is helping her get back to normal. Well, technically, her mother's pills are. The two pill bottles lie side by side on the carpet beside Callie's feet. Callie had read and re-read the labels and made sure Marin only got one of the pills to help her sleep. Callie wants her to sleep though it all. She picks up the other bottle.

Do not take while pregnant. May cause miscarriage.

If two pills "may" cause it, then four would take all uncertainty away. Any moment, the cramping and bleeding would begin. Callie brought up towels.

While Marin sleeps, Callie half-hopes she hears her and so she tells her she loves her. Her hands reach up and caress Marin's cheek and her voice quavers. The boys, they never understand, and they loathe her; she can feel it. But she loathes them right back. She can't imagine wanting them anywhere near her, on her, inside her. She's faintly nauseated at the thought. No, she doesn't want them.

Marin has assured her many times that once she tries boys, she'll like them. Callie doubts it because she's *in love*. It isn't the kind of love that's transient and shallow. It's the real kind, and if only Marin could see that. But Marin does see it and that's the anguish Callie carries in her gut. There's a burning, smoldering place of anger in Callie because Marin simply can't love her back. She can't love her back. Callie, emboldened by the alcohol and her fiery need, places her hand over Marin's breast. She squeezes gently and hears her breathe out faintly. Encouraged, Callie places her leg over Marin's legs and moves closer, close enough to feel her hot breath on Marin's cold cheek.

I love you.

Please love me back.

As if on cue, pain rips through Callie's insides and her eyes fill with tears and fall. She kisses Marin's cheek. Marin's lips are so close and she wants to devour them, so she kisses small pecks around her cheek to her mouth and once there, Callie places her full lips against Marin's. But Marin's lips are cold.

∽

They're all the same.

Cliff, Richard, Hank, and now Garn. Garn asks her about Cliff and she can tell it excites him, knowing she's married to a podiatrist when he's a sales rep for an orthotic company. Probably had a hard on for a doctor's wife for a long time now. But Marilyn went to school with Garn and so did Cliff. Back then he went by Garner.

Garn rubs her palm with his thumb and his breathing deepens.

He's wanted her since high school, he told her. He wasn't playing it right. She wasn't the sexual conquest; he was.

"I have to get home." She gently pulls her hand away.

But then he murmurs in her ear; he figures out the game and Marilyn's hips squirm in small circles as his voice trickles from her ear down, down. He says the right words. She lets his hand move between her legs.

He wants to take her to a hotel. She's too beautiful to be stuck in a car. She approves.

They drive to the closest motel and she stays in the car. He almost bows when he opened the car door.

Once inside the room, he falls to his knees behind her and lifts her dress, worshipping her. Bending her over, she hears him groan as his face invades her pussy. His nose is buried in it, his tongue lapping furiously at her opening.

He continues pleasuring her on his knees and a familiar surrender comes with quaking legs and muscles taut like sinew. He moves away from her and turns her over, slamming her back onto the bed. She's desperate to move the bed spread down—how many other people have fucked on it? But Garn isn't worried about it. Garn growls as he invades her again with his mouth and she allows her squirming to become real.

She maneuvers her dress over her head and he removes his pants, his cock long and stiff, standing between them like a promise.

Marilyn smiles and raises her hips so he can see her open to him. His hand caresses her clit and she quells her helplessness and surrender so that he can see the control in her eyes. She is in control. He does what she wants.

He lies on top of her, rubbing his cock on her clit and she knows Cliff likes this, the smell of 'man' on her body. She imagines him home now, readying himself for her, watching movies and waiting. Instead of inflaming her it douses her, and she closes her eyes. But they fly open as she meets Garn's gaze. His finger invades her ass and it was unexpected. She tightens involuntarily and cramps along with it as unwanted tears threaten. This wasn't what they had discussed; nothing about their meeting suggested it. But maybe this was normal to Garn. She tells herself this as she tries to relax and hold him captive with her stare again but he is in charge and she doesn't know how that happened.

She moves away but he holds her with only a finger and her cry of pain incites his breathing more and his cock continues to stroke her. Soon she feels more pain as he inserts more fingers in her.

Her hips continue to buck and she can't for the life of her decide which way to move. He slides a rubber onto his cock, never taking his fingers out while the pain only increases.

Just relax.

No, no, no this isn't what she wants. She can't control him this way; only her pussy controls them and she tries to scoot away from him but he holds her. The moment of relief as his fingers slip out of her ass is short-lived because his cock invades her, tears into her, and she screams. All she can think of now is the safety of Cliff and how she has no right to ask for his protection, his understanding, or his sympathy when she'd come to this motel room like a hungry whore.

Her opening and body scream in pain along with her voice and he tells her to be quiet and relax and she can't move now because he's in her ass, all the way, and her body surrenders for its own good.

His finger finds her clit and massages and she doesn't want him to make her come again. She doesn't because it gives him permission to violate her and she can't be a victim of his if she comes. But come she does—in a shuddering cry and he eggs her on by complimenting her *tight little asshole* and it's no compliment at all because everyone has one like hers and she's not special to him and she knows it.

She bucks him backward in one desperate jerk and he slides out of her with a cry. His face contorts and his semen sprays all over her torso and into her mouth, her face, her hair. Her throat seizes up and the smell isn't of sex and lust but of his garlic pasta and his corrupted, salty manhood and she gags as she smells it in her hair. She tries to move completely out from under him, but can't; his repugnantly dark, hairy body is suddenly an embodiment of the smell and she gags again and turns her face away.

She can't decide whether to get in the shower to wash him off or to vomit, but his body traps her there and her legs protest impotently.

Sweat forms on her upper lip as she wipes his fluid away. Her appearance doesn't matter, now. He's seen the inside of her, the ugliest parts. She awaits his discovery of her here, under him, bleeding and violated and sated all at once, and then her phone vibrates and she realizes it's been going off since they arrived.

To die, to sleep,
No more; and by a sleep to say we end
The heart-ache, and the thousand natural shocks
That flesh is heir to: 'tis a consummation
Devoutly to be wished. To die, to sleep;
To sleep, perchance to dream – ay, there's the rub:
For in that sleep of death what dreams may come,
When we have shuffled off this mortal coil,
Must give us pause – there's the respect
That makes calamity of so long life.
~William Shakespeare

PART III

October, 2010

1

It's easier with her now. There has been enough talk, enough intimacy. But not once has he entered her and he won't think about that as she removes her suit coat and reveals the slightly damp back of her work dress shirt.

All dressed up and nowhere to go.

Cliff smiles and thinks of the alternate saying. She has someone to blow today. His cock stirs. Chelle casts a flirtatious glance behind her as she walks to the bathroom with a sway in her gait. Now is the time for Cliff to get hard, get ready. She'll come out naked, those hips moving, her warm cunt beckoning him to plunge inside. He quivers and pulls his pants open. The noise from the bathroom catches his attention and with his turgid dick resting in his palm he walks towards the noise.

The shower curtain's clear and he sees her dark skin, her curvy shape, moving in the water. It's as though she moves to music only she can hear and he can't move to any music; he can't move at all. He wants to shout to her to get out. Moisture builds on his upper lip and the steam plays tricks on his lungs and he can't take a breath.

She is no longer a woman, but a vision—a ghostly visitation just for him and he stuffs his limp cock back into his pants and pushes himself toward the shower curtain.

But his hand won't rise to open it. He sees her white teeth smiling at him, and she shares her tune, humming as she dances. But the baring of teeth is all he sees and the figure of the dead girl swimming on his floor, the blue, floral blanket encircling them like wreathes. Unconscious, half-naked, no longer hard, no longer warm, no longer moist, but cold and life-less and vacant and the sob reaches past his throat and he turns, staggers, and runs.

The stairs seem monumental as she stops, for the second time, on them. *The box is not that heavy.*

Marilyn berates herself and thinks of her protein intake. Has she had enough today? Or is it every day? The fatigue, it seems, sets in by 10 a.m. and she must rest. She's missed her afternoon Pilates class twice this week. She pulls the box up pushing with her legs and walks the last two stairs. The box 'thunks' down onto the floor on the main level.

The pain has been something with which she's lived for days now, but today it encircles her waist like a long, lost friend. Today, as she kneels on the carpet next to her Thanksgiving box, it's as though familiar pincers compress her insides and the feeling is almost a comfort. Like coming home.

She moves along the carpet on her side and finally stops at the couch. She lifts herself up and the knives in her belly double her over and it's only then she has the sense to be afraid.

Marilyn licks her upper lip and tastes the salty sweat on it. The shak-ing in her hands will quell in time. She knows it because it always does. It happened this way with the laundry baskets last week. It happens this way when she has PMS. And she does. Relief floods her, even though on some level she knew it all along. The cramping, the pain, the fatigue. Yes, all of it made sense now.

She smiles and holds her middle like an infant and cradles it.

I am a woman, still. I'm just a woman.

He hears the air shift around him as if a tide sucks out the last of the frothy sea. Murmurs ripple through the warehouse and Dan glances up briefly before going back to invoices. The golden blond hair catches his eye and he sucks in a breath as he sees Callie Erickson approach his office. Mounting the stairs, she takes a fleeting glimpse around her.

Before standing, he searches out the faces of the men milling about. He knows they are sharks, circling the fresh meat, and he jumps up from his desk and practically lunges for the door.

"Callie?"

"Hi, Mr. Shaw…Dan."

"What are you doing here?"

"Didn't you get my message?"

"No, no message, Callie."

Callie is wearing black slacks that conform to her body, and a white shirt that shows a lacy white bra underneath. His face reddens as he shifts his eyes away.

"I left one for you last night. The guy on the phone said I could come in today and talk to you about work."

"Why would you need to talk about work?" he says, stymied. Then it hits him. "About—about you working…*here*?"

"Well, yeah. Office work or…"

"Callie, I'm not the guy you'd talk to about that." He instantly moves closer as he feels the stares from the men in the warehouse, their hungry eyes devouring her in his fishbowl office. He lowers his voice. "Who did you talk to? I mean, it's not a big deal. I can put in a word, point you in the right direction…"

"You could just hire me." He sees Marilyn in her now; decisive, direct, coy, all at once.

"Callie, I can't."

He's sincere on so many levels. He can't even look at her normally, and yet his co-workers lascivious stares make him physically grow to cover her from their hungry eyes. He moves in front of her, closer, and he can smell her sweet perfume, almost like cotton candy, and he's reminded of how sweet cotton candy is, baby pink, then darker from the wetness of his mouth.

He licks his dry lips and stares into her round eyes as they darken.

"Why? Is it because I'm a girl? I mean, a female?"

"No...no..." but that's exactly why and he knows that she's both woman and girl for him and if he had to see her every day she would forever be the thread in his fabric of sanity that would unravel, bit by bit. "That's not why."

"Then what is it?"

"I'm not hiring anyone at this warehouse."

"That's not what the guy on the phone said last night."

Dan is itching to find out who the fuck worked phones last night and why the fuck he didn't inform him of any of this.

"Was his name Geary? The guy you—"

"Look, I know why you won't hire me. I get it. I'm leaving. So much for 'if there's anything I can do to help you out, Callie.' Right?"

Had he said that to her? He reaches out and his hand collides with her arm, soft and fragrant, and he wants to pull back but he can't now. He holds her arm like that and shuts his eyes. "Don't leave, Callie. Have a seat. You want coffee? I can get you coffee."

"No, I don't want coffee. I want a real job. School sucks and I'm sick of learning shit I'll never use."

It's easier for him now. He can see the petulant child in her and the invisible hands that began squeezing his shoulders from the moment she walked in ease up on him. He takes his seat safely behind his desk.

"Callie, don't quit school. You don't wanna end up like those losers out there, do ya? Or like me? Right?" He smiles, his charm visible like the dimple in the corner of his mouth.

"You do okay, right?"

"I had to go through years of shit to get here, Callie. You don't want to have to kiss ass and—"

"And what?"

"It's just really back-breaking. Literally. That's why I don't throw freight anymore. My back went out."

"It did?"

"Yeah, it did."

A small crease forms on her perfect brow, an innocent glimpse of how tender she can be. "I'm sorry. But my back is strong."

She shrugs in slow motion and her breasts seem to bounce on a sea of luminescent waves and he can't for the life of him even remember what they are talking about.

"What does your mom or dad say?"

He's aware he said "or". He can't put them together, even verbally. Marilyn has ignored his calls for two weeks.

"I'm an adult. They really don't get a say in what I do anymore." She smiles and her head drops but her eyes stay on him, unnervingly.

"Callie, you don't wanna work here."

"No, you don't *want* me to work here."

"Why would I—"

"You can't stand seeing me at all, can you."

"It was a long time ago."

"I'm talking about *now*."

"Now?"

"I'm talking about my mother."

Dan holds very still, as if he's in water and any movement would attract predator. Callie leans over onto the desk, eyes tilted up to meet his.

"I've *seen* you."

Dan only shakes his head. Callie nods, eyes never leaving him. He bows his head down.

"I have. You were in the car in my garage. My dad was in Los Angeles…"

"I don't know what you're saying." His eyes study the desk in front of him. He knows he can't deny it and make it stick. Not with her. He and Marilyn had heard the door close that night.

"The headlights were still on. I saw your face. I saw *her*." The last part comes out raw, grating along his skin. He'd expected her anger to be for him.

"Callie—"

"C'mon, go with me on this, Dan. All you have to do is nod your head."

His nostrils flare but he stays frozen, as if made of ice and steel. The wood grain in his desk undulates like waves. Movement catches his eye and when he looks up, her whole demeanor has changed, softened. She's become liquescent and her shoulders rise up to her ears as she leans on his desk with both forearms flat, fingers splayed. Her shirt opening inches toward the lacy white bra, and he doesn't look away. He's mesmerized by the surge of honey-golden flesh welling up over the edge. Her voice deepens.

"Haven't you ever wanted to fuck a younger version of her?"

His head snaps to the side in a panic, as if other ears will hear. When he meets her gaze, his head shakes 'no' almost imperceptibly. The office's silence is punctuated by his breathing and his white knuckles hold onto the arms of his chair like a life raft.

"You need to go." His hoarse whisper is so quiet he can hear the noises from the warehouse encroach in his office like a torrent. She stares at him for a moment longer and then shrugs as she straightens.

"Don't worry. I haven't told my dad."

She leaves him there, swimming in a pool of his own perspiration. She leaves him there thinking about the mother and the daughter.

***

Pin-prickly sensations spread as gooseflesh appears on her freshly shaved legs. Chelle doesn't bother to dry them. She only holds the towel in front of her breasts, as if she's afraid an assault will come straight for her heart.

Tip-toeing out of the bathroom, she visually confirms what she'd heard. Cliff has bolted, yes. Soon, shivering crawls up her legs and into her torso. Teeth chattering, she sits quietly on the bed.

Motherfucker. *Mother. Fucker.*

Her hand absently rubs her soft belly and she imagines her hand is a claw as she grasps her flesh painfully to wake herself. Angry black tears create grotesque lines on her cheeks. The mascara is new. Bought yesterday at lunch. Preparing for him. She lets a small shriek of anger escape her lips.

The liquor store is next to the motel.

The fiery liquid is the only fire that calms her rage and she can almost taste it as it burns all the way down, but without it the rage remains, always. She stares into her eyes in the reflective glass on the picture of red buttes, her face hidden behind angry black bars.

Motherfucker.

With a rattle, the air conditioner slogs to life and tendrils of her cold hair turn her back numb. Her breath huffs out and her feet dance on the carpet, jittery and taut.

He ran home to *her. Cunt, whore.*

Or did he run *from* Chelle? Cliff got the full visual of her ample breasts and round belly and wide hips and—no. She wouldn't listen to her father's voice tell her she had her mother's plump body. She would not listen to him tell her she looked like a fat rutting pig when he caught her with Marco Perez.

She would only listen to her mother *cluck cluck* and pinch her and tell her that real men liked curvaceous and meaty bodies to hold and have till death do they part or until they die of asphyxiation in their own bile.

Marin's body had been starting to gain that meaty form and Chelle had disapproved, but it was only to protect her. Men know what lurks underneath those short skirts and low-cut blouses. Chelle's job had been to shield her daughter because she *knew*. She knew what those evil pigs thought about her baby when she walked by them.

'Marin Manuela, why do you dress like a whore? Look at those shorts! Go put on some goddamned clothes!'

'But everyone has these shorts—'

'Not everyone fills them out the way you fill them out. Go change your clothes—now!'

'*No*! It's not—'

And Chelle told her with a swift smack to her face that you do not argue with your mother.

If Marin was alive, she would be thanking her now. She would thank her for telling her she looked like a whore. She would know that curvy women are labeled and identified by their very own flesh; their own bodies betray them.

But she isn't alive and Chelle's hands ache from gripping the coverlet on the bed.

"Stupid...*fucking whore!*"

There. She'd said it. Her daughter could take it now, hear how she had hurt and disappointed and ruined everything with her selfishness. In defiance of Marin's memory, she shrieks it to the ceiling.

The towel drops to the floor and her wide hips tell her that she is a whore, too. She sits on the bed, still soaking wet. Her body is a string, strained over an open wound, ready to play a tearful ballad with undertones of rage. She rages over a man who is pale and vapid. He isn't used to mounds of flesh. He's used to bone and sand and sinew. He's used to her. She rages over being abandoned by all of them.

Marin would have had her child by now. Chelle thinks of the small hands and wide brown eyes and how her own child would be a little younger than Marin's baby had she chose to let it live. It would have been so very complicated, all of those brown eyes looking up to her.

Chelle stands and finds her clothes, dressing slow and methodical as she reasons it through. Each pant leg, each arm hole, is a child and all of her children have died on her watch, under her wing. Three dead, and none of them can point a finger at her and say that she'd done it to them.

But she had. The final sleeve of her blouse hangs loose and open and she forces her hand through, believing that the final child is her. The silk blouse rips on her ring and she doesn't bother to inspect it. Silky cloth caresses her arm and it's the soft flesh of Marin's face. Chelle wonders why the only tactile memory she has of Marin is the impact on her palm from her silken cheek.

The touch was too brief to recall it. The touch was too brief to really feel her skin. Chelle only remembers how it stung her palm and how the strike ripped Marin's gaze in two.

And her black tears make way for fresh ones that streak down. The black tears are washed away and cleansed, consecrating her face. The shape of her mouth contorts to her sobs and one hand tentatively reaches out for her reflection, desperate to caress a cheek that is no longer there.

2

Ryanne has an ink smudge on her face.

Callie wants to wipe at it, more out of irritation rather than tenderness. Her arms stay at her sides as Ryanne blows smoke away from her.

"So how've you been?"

"Busy." Callie nods. "Finals are coming up."

"Yeah, I know. I just finished. So… why are you here."

"I dunno. I mean, I thought—"

"Are you ever sober? God, I can smell it on you a mile away."

"I had two beers. *Two.*"

Ryanne shrugs and looks away. Callie steps closer. "Look, I'm trying."

"To what? Drink yourself to death?"

"Oh, you've been talking to my mother, now, huh?"

"Jesus. What do you want, Callie?"

Callie doesn't like hearing her name from Ryanne. She likes the nickname Ryanne had given her and to hear her real name stabs at her insides. She'd had more than two beers. She fumbles in her purse for gum.

"I thought we were friends."

Ryanne huffs out and kicks the ground with her sneaker. "I thought we would be more. But, whatever. You're way too confused."

"I'm not confused. I—I'm not. I mean I was…but now I'm not." Callie moves closer and presses her cheek to Ryanne's. Her gaze moves behind Ryanne's head to the power lines stretching across a fiery orange sky. Her vision blurs slightly and the lines begin to move, waving to her, calling her, electric arms encircling her.

Ryanne's lips are so close to hers and she closes her eyes but when she opens them, all she sees are power lines moving, undulating in the waning light. The lines reach out to her, seem closer than before and with each movement of Ryanne's hands, lips, legs, Callie hears the buzz of currents shooting through her.

They smell different. Marin never smelled of cigarettes and sandalwood. Marin's smell was like sweet coconut and reticent lilies with closed, moist petals. Callie was used to that smell and even now, four years later, she can still conjure up that sweet scent of Marin's body and hair. Ryanne's foreign smell, almost masculine, dulls her head even as her languid touch and tongue electrifies her.

The rear of the print shop where Ryanne works is deserted and cinder block scratches the back of Callie's head as Ryanne's mouth probes hers fervently, as if to bring her to life. Callie is more afraid to back out now, so she focuses on the sky as Ryanne's hands explore her. If she keeps her eyes closed she can almost smell sweet lilies in Ryanne's hair. This illusion alone awakens Callie's body and she reciprocates Ryanne's kiss with an urgency that startles them both.

Lights in the parking lot spring to life and Callie buries her face in Ryanne's hair even as sounds echo down the small alley where they stand. Callie definitely smells lilies and she wants to cry. Ryanne pulls back to gaze at her.

"Where are you?"

Callie shakes her head imperceptibly. "I'm here."

"Why do you seem so far away then?"

Callie looks to the side. "We're in public. I mean, anyone could—"

"Can I see you tonight? I'm off at ten."

Callie nods and Ryanne's teeth dazzle her with a wide smile. Ryanne kisses her quickly and walks away, gravel crunching under her feet. Callie can still taste the smoke in her mouth.

She stands in the same spot, never wanting to leave, never wanting to lose the smell of Ryanne's hair because it's now amalgamated with Marin's and she is the one Callie wants to touch. Marin is the one Callie sees in the evening sky, while power lines stay perfectly still, silent and aloof, no longer beckoning her to come.

∾

They'd been overtly polite at The Center, but she sees the hurt in Dan's eyes and she knows it's time they talk. The thrill of knowing he still wants her tugs on her, but so does the fear.

Dan holds the front door open and she's taken aback at the stylish apartment, the way the chilly air immediately cools her skin.

"Nice place."

"I'm house-sitting for my sister while she's in Europe. I gotta find a permanent place in a couple months."

"I see. Well, it's nice, anyway."

The subject of his split with his wife is too volatile for Marilyn to touch. The air shifts around her; moisture and heat blossom between her legs as she feels Dan close in on her. His breath touches the back of her neck.

"I've missed you." His voice is husky, deep, straining against his throat like his need strains through his pants. She feels it against her lower back and shuts her eyes.

"Dan..."

"Where have you been? Why haven't you returned my calls?"

"I've been busy. I've had to think things through."

"I love you."

"Dan..."

"What?" He clasps her arm and pivots her toward him. "Is it Cliff?"

"Is *what* Cliff?"

"Why you haven't called."

Marilyn studies his eyes. There are so many nuances to his question. Her vision moves down to his lips. *Is it Cliff?* She reconstructs the past few weeks with her husband and it all coalesces in a blur of turned backs and perfunctory comments. Her eyes no longer focus, but she hears Dan's breathing deepen and she inhales to answer.

"Cliff is…my husband."

"Yeah, and why is that? You can't tell me you're happy with him!"

Dan's grip on her arm is vise-like and it's as though the fingers clasp around her throat, compress her lungs. Dan would never understand the way Cliff understands her.

"It's not Cliff the way you think it's Cliff."

She moves back from Dan but his grip tightens. He steps closer and his mouth covers hers and she panics for lack of air and space. She turns her head away and he moves her chin back toward him.

"Or is it someone else." The look in his eyes is dark. This is the part where she coyly denies, wide-eyed, while Cliff takes her and thrusts every detail out of her as if two men penetrate her and fuck her at once. This is where she and Cliff fuck them together and for one brief moment they commiserate in nameless accord.

But Dan doesn't share. She knows this and it stirs both panic and craving for some rich, warm flood to consume her. In her mind she imagines a life with only one man. Dan is her suitor now. As a husband, would he treat her as an exotic, untouchable prize? Would she still be able to be the elusive prey who needs to be pursued?

No. Dan requires a partner and it's then that Marilyn pulls back because it's then that she sees what she can't be. To Dan.

To Cliff. To anyone. Rather than being liberating, her heart painfully lurches and enters blackness. Then Dan makes it easy.

"Who is it? *Tell me!*" He yanks her arm, moving her toward him and she rolls like a rag doll, taking her licks, but then her spine stiffens and she steps away.

"Does it matter? It isn't you." Her icy anger at his presumption laces her words and she sees the bewilderment on his face transform into actual shock. He never saw this coming. She had been his savior, his illumination after a long sleep. Now, she harshly sets him free to fend for himself. For his own good. It's the kindest thing she could do.

"Bullshit."

"What's bullshit?"

"You're choosing him over me. What is it? Money? What's the payoff, Mar?"

"Go to hell."

"Oh, that's right, you're the Ice Queen, no passion except when you're grinding your hips into me and even then it's controlled!"

His assessment shuts her down her mind. Her responses turn into gray, static fuzz.

"You have no idea what I'm about—what you're even talking about!"

"Don't I? I've given up everything for you! Chelle knows—she's going to divorce me. What was I to you? What am I to you?"

"What am I to *you*? That's the million dollar question, Dan. You say you love me but we've never had a conversa—"

"I've shared my very soul with you! But you're right. It's been one-sided all along, hasn't it? I tell you how I grieve over my daughter and you tell me exactly *dick* about you."

"There's no *room* to talk to you about me—you're so consumed with your Catholic guilt and anger and grief, you can't hear anything I say!"

His eyes search her face and he turns and walks to the edge of a chair. He leans against it and bows his head, shaking it.

"You don't let me in." His chin lifts and his stare is cold. "I'm not imagining that."

"I want to! I—I want to but I can't!" Her tears burst from her and her face crumples. "How can I complain to you when *she's gone*?"

The blame, the pain, spoken out loud, but without a name to complete it. "*She*" is the only way Marilyn can refer to Marin. Dan's shoulders slump, but his eyes blaze.

"You used to be a reminder, did you know that? Every time I saw you at The Center, my heart would just...fucking..."

"I'm sorry," she whispers.

"No...don't be. You knew it and you healed it. My heart's whole because of you...can't you see that?"

"No, it isn't. You mourn fresh every day."

"You help me heal every day!"

"I can't help you anymore!"

"Why! Tell me why, goddamnit! You're my—" his voice cracks and he bows his head again, sniffing.

"I don't have what it takes to heal you anymore."

He stands and steps toward her, taking her in his arms. "Then let *me* heal *you*." His mouth covers hers and for just a brief moment, she allows her body to melt into him. Then she extracts herself from him.

"Don't you see? You're a reminder for me, too."

"What? What do I remind you of?"

Her tears pool in her eyes and she opens her mouth to speak. Nothing comes for a few beats. Finally:

"Failure."

∽

What was the matter with him that he hadn't thought of it for so long? He doesn't even recall thinking on it the night it happened.

The sight of Chelle seemed to inject the event into his brain and he's suddenly sick with it. How he'd almost lost his baby. How Chelle had lost hers. And now, the sick fuck that he is, he's been seeing her. He's been trying to fuck the mother of the girl who died in his house.

He blinks rapidly and scours the intersections for cars, praying to God Chelle hasn't followed him to his office. What could he possibly say to her that was true?

It has been four years. The memory of it caves in on him and his trembling lips mouth the words he's so wanted to say.

I'm sorry. I'm so sorry.

It was a mix-up. An accident. He had thought it was Marilyn in his shower.

He ignores the taunts in his mind that he knows better—knew better then, and did nothing but stand in the bathroom lusting after a child.

I had been drinking.

But you knew.

I couldn't see.

But you knew.

And hours later she was gone. Even now he can't think about the death, only the inadvertent violation in the bathroom and what, if any, part it had played.

How long had he stood there? One minute? Three?

Too long.

Too fucking long.

If it had only been one minute would she still be alive?

He orients himself, startled back into the present. How long had he been driving? Ten minutes? Thirty? He glances around and makes a quick U-turn amidst shrieking tires and horns.

Back at his office, he exits his car and he slams the door closed, as if he hopes to shut the rancid thoughts tightly inside. But they follow him, dogging him as his damp shirt peels itself from his back with his stride.

His assistant, Heidi, stands behind the seated receptionist and her eyes question him. He's 20 minutes late.

"We were just going to call—"

"Sorry I'm late." He doesn't look at them for fear they will see his sin on his countenance. He knows this is silly. He needs time—time to think. He needs time to exonerate himself. If he could just have five minutes, he'll be alright.

Right as rain.

Walking back to his office, he closes the door behind him. He leans against his desk, safely away from everyone who would take a chunk from him. The weight of so many people and thoughts bear on him. His neck stiffens with the heaviness. As his back chills, he wonders why the rooms are so cold. Just because it's hot outside doesn't mean it has to be an arctic tundra inside. He'd explain this to Heidi. She is the only woman who will ever understand him. And he pays her to understand.

He hears a car pull up outside and he leaps for the window, peeking through the blinds.

No, Chelle isn't one to follow. She has dignity. And him? He has nothing. The self-derision seems apropos now as he lets everyone down around him.

A knock at the door and his eyes close.

"Dr. Erickson?"

"Come in, Heidi."

Her face, seemingly disembodied, floats around the door. Her smile is expectant. "Are you alright?"

He allows a small smile to glance on his lips. He doesn't pay her to ask that. "Yes. I am. Is our 2 o'clock here?"

"Yes. But you have some wiggle room because there's no one at two-thirty."

He has a fifteen minute reprieve. He glances at the couch and stifles a yawn. "Okay. Two minutes. Bring her back to a room."

Heidi, normally efficient and task oriented, freezes in the doorway. Her look is questioning. "Doctor? You...seem tired."

"Do I?"

"A little." She looks around uncomfortably because this is the closest they've ever been to a two-way conversation.

"Thank you, Heidi."

She smiles a soft smile and nods her head, then eases the door closed. Cliff thinks that Heidi would make a good wife. She is round and ordinary and would want to be with him. She would cook for him, and when the time came, she would ask him if he's alright.

∽

Callie's gaze settles on the four-step staircase that leads into the attic. *Her room.* The closed door looms ahead. With one foot on the first step, she flips on the light, then continues up.

At the top of the stairs, she opens the door to the shadowy room. The waning light of evening does nothing to illuminate the space. She glances over at the tower of boxes partially covering the window. The room had been invaded over the last four years by storage: wreaths, old clothes, books, photos in need of assembly into albums. A trunk filled with spare blankets sits against the wall.

Her room.

After Marin died she couldn't spend time in it again. She had only gone in briefly and on rare occasions when Marilyn requested something out of storage. She always thought Marilyn made her go on purpose, to make her suffer.

And she ought to suffer.

More boxes have been added to the mix over the past year. They sit one atop the other like bricks in a wall, a wall to keep her from revisiting her past. Callie slides past a stack of plastic bins, and comes to a stack of liquor store boxes. She leans against them, pushing with all of her might. The boxes hold books; there would be no moving them en masse. She pulls the top one off and balances it in her arms as she shuffles along a narrow opening between the containers. She places it against the far wall, away from the window. The second box is easier and the third easier still. The room brightens as boxes line the walls instead of standing in the center like forbidding mountains.

She'd come up to find the errant photographs of the distant past and instead, she excavates for another past. The past they all forget while they wander the halls of their house like strangers.

Callie can almost see right through the last two boxes onto the floor. Marin's blood had soaked through the towels and blanket. She remembers seeing it and reaching for her hand; she remembers the screams. The screams weren't from Marin, though, because she'd been so still and peaceful and then they hauled her away while steel arms held Callie down and hands fluttered over her. Callie hadn't screamed either. Her voice, a soft whisper, had told Marin to hold her, to not let them take her away. Rough thumbs held her eyes open while a blinding light encompassed her vision—more screaming, then blackness.

Callie stares at the boxes, wondering how the stain looks now, what color resides in her mother's light taupe carpet. She pulls the box off with a purposeful tug, relishing the moment, eyes wide and shiny with tears. Callie stacks the box and stops to gaze at her fingers, slightly red from the cardboard handles.

Her hand burns with the feeling of Marin's silky hair under it. She wants to tell Marin she's sorry, that she'd tried to come with her. Callie gave her one too many. Maybe two. She didn't know. Callie sees the pills drop in Marin's hand. One, two, three…would three have been enough? What if Callie had stopped Marin at three? What if Callie hadn't stopped herself at five? What if six sleeping pills would have done it? *Just one more…*

Her hand blurs in front of her and she brings it up to wipe her face. The hospital room had been so cold.

Callie, can you count to ten for me?

One, two, three…where's Marin?

Callie, do you remember how many pills you took?

I—no, no—where's Marin!

They'd all held the same look on their faces, like her query baffled them. Callie had to scream at them to make them tell her.

The final box sits on the floor and it's small so she can't understand why she can't see the stain yet. Her breathing deepens, and her heart slams against her ribs as she reaches her foot out and moves the box away from her. The carpet darkens only slightly as the plush fibers go against the grain. She can see where the box resided, but there is no stain.

No, no, no! Where…? I have… to see Marin…

You can't see her, she's gone.

Callie collapses on the carpet and shoves the box violently away from her until it slams against the wall. She runs her hands over the carpet and the piling feels the same. No color, no stiffness, no trace. She pulls the box toward her and awkwardly maneuvers it behind her and she sprawls her upper body over the invisible stain. She can't catch her breath as sobs wrack her body. Callie scrambles to the trunk and flings it open. Rummaging through the blankets, the blue one with flowers is not there. They could have washed it, made it new again, and Callie would have looked at it and remembered Marin's dark hair.

Like a house that had been cleared of spirits, the trunk holds nothing of Marin, nothing of Callie. She returns to the carpet and runs her hands all over it, clawing at the fibers, trying to feel any discrepancy.

She raises her head up quickly, tears dousing her face, and snaps her neck to her left. Crawling over to a bag of clothes and a wreath box, she grabs at them and flings them behind her. Her gaze narrows onto the floor.

She had always burned incense and the ash had invariably dropped on the carpet, leaving black dots all over it.

As she peers closely at the area on the carpet, the only thing she sees is loose carpet piling from the edges. The truth is confirmed. She tears at the new carpet with her fingers, intent on ripping it up to see the floor underneath. Surely the floor has a small vestige of her and Marin. But the glue and nails hold firm.

Small noises emit from her as she prostrates herself on the floor. She slowly curls into a ball.

Her mother's face, wretched and crunched up like a raisin, stares down at her and she can't talk to her because there's plastic in her mouth and in her nose and machines in the room sighing like sleeping giants. Her fingers move and reach for the rail and then her father's hand covers hers and tells her she will be alright. Her hand continues to move because in moving she would make them understand that she only wanted to be with Marin; the rest was unnecessary. But they couldn't hear her. They were replacing the carpet and burning blankets and carting Marin down a long hall while they ran with her in the other direction.

Callie sees the gurney retreat from her and no one can hear her scream through the plastic mask. Her hand reaches and the IV pulls and more steel arms move across her. They don't understand that from underneath the white sheet retreating from her, her blue, flower blanket dangles down and they need to uncover Marin's face so she can see her. She just needs to see her and tell her she's sorry, she's so sorry.

Then without warning, Callie sleeps.

3

Chelle's eyes are glittery glass, moisture hovering on her lower lids. But it isn't because Dan's asked her if he can come home. She's *in a mood*—that is to say, she's had wine. Every type of alcohol comes out of her differently. Wine gives her those glittery-glass eyes, like a serpent watching a small animal root for food near its den.

The corners of her mouth slope down. This means she's had more than three glasses. But he can't talk to her about that.

Dan clears his throat and turns his palms up. "Well? You haven't—"

"Why." She doesn't ask. She throws it out—an accusation. Her hand reaches for her glass and Dan makes the first serious mistake of the evening: his eyes dart to the table where the wine glass sits. "What? You have a problem with me having a glass of wine?"

"I didn't say that."

She huffs out a bitter laugh. "You didn't have to." She chugs the remainder of her wine and stares at him, through him, defiantly. He reaches for the bottle.

"More wine?"

"Don't fucking patronize me."

"Jesus Christ." Dan leans backward into his chair and gazes at the ceiling. It's the safest place to look. He hears her pick up the bottle and pour.

"I don't want any, thanks." Dan smiles.

"I didn't offer."

"Yes—yes I know that. I was being droll."

"Oh, that's right, you're the funny guy. Lemme ask you, Funny Guy, did you make her laugh?"

He hadn't expected Chelle to immediately welcome him home. But this evening seems to be a twisted exercise in how to make him as uncomfortable as possible. He should have seen it coming.

"I wanna talk about us, Chelle."

"I wanna talk about *her*, Dan." Her laugh is lurid with her glittery eyes. He almost stands to leave. But he's taken much more than this over the years.

"I'd rather not—"

"I don't care what you'd *rather*, Dan. Ha—like the news guy. Ironic."

Dan doesn't ask her why it's ironic.

Chelle raises her eyes to the ceiling with a cruel smile on her face. Her tongue traces her upper lip and Dan remembers being enthralled by this gesture of hers once upon a time; now it looks obscene. "How was she? Did she scream? Was she a screamer, Dan?"

He swallows heavily and looks away. His insides, still tender from the loss, recoil. He makes his second fatal mistake.

"I said I don't want to talk about her. It—it's over. That's all you need to know."

"Wrong! I need to know everything!" Chelle slams her glass on the table and wine sloshes over the side. Falling out of her chair onto her knees, she moves in front of him with her fingers digging into his legs. "I want to know how she smelled, tasted, felt…I wanna know if you fucked her up against a building."

He clenches his eyes closed. "Chelle, stop—"

Her voice lowers seductively. "Did you fuck her from behind? Did you eat her? Tell me about her magical cunt that you loved so much, Dan. Did she suck you till you came? I want to know. I want to know if you came in her—"

"Stop it—"

"—I wanna know if you liked the way she tasted—"

"—God, Chelle, *enough*—"

"I want to know if *you made her fucking laugh*!" Her voice echoes throughout the empty house.

He opens his eyes, ready to end it, ready to stand and walk out, never look back. His breath catches in his throat as his gaze alights on his wife's face. It's contorted in an agonized grimace while tears stream down her cheeks. Dan sees the wounds he alone caused and his hands rise up to touch her. They hover in mid-air, trembling as her claw-like fingers dig deeper into his flesh.

Her teeth are tinged purple with the wine and her whole body shudders, as if wracked internally with a torrent while the floodgates outside barely hold the deluge. She breathes through her mouth, causing her whole face to quaver with each inhale, each exhale.

Dan watches her face silently and tries to conjure Marilyn's composed visage, the cool veneer to Chelle's ferocity. Her porcelain cheeks and delicate bones, translucent eyes, and perfumed neck contrasts wildly now with his wife and he wonders when the other became more compelling.

His history with Chelle coagulates before him and as it does he grasps her face in between his hands, forcing her to stare at him. Hot tears seep from his eyes and the release causes his mouth to open slightly.

"Never," he whispers. "I never made her laugh."

Chelle's body wracks convulsively with a final sob, and then she slips from him like a bead of viscous liquid, pooling onto the floor.

⁓

The soft, downy hair of Dan's arm tickles her fingers as she brushes it. His snore is mellifluous, almost a whisper; it comforts her while she watches the ceiling move to the right, stop, and start over. It never ceases to amaze her, the tricks her eyes can play when she has wine.

Rather than sleep, Chelle longs for the cool air of the night on her face and suddenly she must have it. She rolls out of Dan's grasp and sits on the side of the bed to get her bearings. It's much less pleasant to see the wall tip before her. She blinks to clear her vision and stands, swaying slightly.

She's careful as she descends the stairs, moving delicately although she knows Dan won't wake. He sleeps like the dead after he comes.

The house is all shadow with familiar lumps of darkness congregated in the familiar spots: the chair, couch, papa san. She knows where the table is.

If she goes out to the back yard the dog will accost her. She'll hardly be alone. Dogs are, in some respects, needier than infants. And he might bark. She walks across the carpet and her feet touch the cold tile of the entry way before the front door.

The handle is smooth and icy and suddenly she can't turn the knob. Darkness, like an oppressive glove, pushes her back from the door. A familiar vise grips her gut, and there is only one thing that quiets the impending doom.

The bottle of wine still rests on the table in the living room. Although it's only a shadow, she knows what it holds, and the threat of the darkness is, for the moment, held at bay.

∽

"It's not possible. Is it?"

The first surprise had come when she'd found the pregnancy tests in Callie's bathroom cupboard. Marilyn knew Callie had been sexually active. The package had been unopened—until now.

Marilyn counts her dates and her consternation turns into disbelief. Then shock. Then she gets sick.

The icy side of the tub digs into her back as she sits on the floor of her bathroom. Her legs stretch out before her as she stares at the lines on the plastic test wand. Two red lines.

She had not been able to conceive after having Callie. Then after the cancer, she had only one ovary left. Surgery on her cervix and uterine lining made pregnancy a very slim possibility. They said unless it healed well, she'd never be able to carry a child to term.

Marilyn stands and peels off her shirt and her bra. She cups her breasts and squeezes. They don't feel sore. Her period is at least three weeks late. She's had all of the signs it would start. Then nothing. She thinks back and realizes that her last period had only lasted a couple of days.

Dan.

He's the one she wants to tell. She feels, deep down, that this baby, if she's indeed pregnant, is his. A romantic notion perhaps. Something to bind them together, just as Callie's presence is something which tears she and Cliff apart. She had said good-bye to Dan and for what? *For what.* Maybe it's time she grew up and settled down. But no...

Her breasts do feel fuller, however. Come to think of it. She looks down and catches her breath.

Normally she holds her tummy in as a habit. As she gazes down, she sees the small mound rising out of her jeans.

"Oh my God, oh my God..."

She paces with her hand held up to her forehead. Her stomach has been touchy; she has been exhausted. Moody. Irritable. She looks into the mirror and her face holds shock, but something else, too. Light has drifted into her eyes and without thinking, she places her hand across her tummy and rubs.

She would, of course, need to take the other pregnancy test. This could be a false positive. But those are so rare now. *So rare...*

Marilyn rubs her hand down the sides of her face and dares a smile; she blinks back tears. It would be a miracle. But in the end, who would it save?

She can't answer that question now because a burst of energy invades her. Her mind wanders to the office down the hall. It's next to Callie's room. Callie might move out and then the baby...

The baby. The baby could have Callie's room. The thrill of it quickens her heart and it almost hurts. Almost. Cliff's face. She imagines Cliff's face as she tells him they are having a baby. No, she couldn't tell him just yet. Dan? The very fact that it could be either man's child doesn't quash her excitement. She knows it's crazy, she knows it's impossible. She also knows that she has never given up hope.

And when she thinks of Dan, her chest clenches painfully. She knows that feeling, that feeling she gets when one man has her. That settles it.

It could not possibly be Cliff's baby because Cliff has nothing to give her. He, by his very nature, is insipid and stale. He is too removed from her to impregnate her. He always has been. She can't imagine his virility reached all the way into his body to produce sperm. *No.* His light hair, light smile, light hands…the way he patiently moves in and out of her while asking her if she's fucked someone else, all of this negates his virtue.

That's not how babies are made.

Dan has fire for blood and ruts in her like an animal, desperate to crawl inside her tiny space and take root. He had even mentioned having a child one day. But she had been dozing and dismissed it. She dismissed it because he had missed Marin so terribly that day and her warm embrace had cured him, if only for the moment. Dan had shot himself into her and when the condom broke that one time, they'd given them up. Dan was overcome with this gesture of hers, to let him inside, unsheathed. It was proof to him that she was his, that she wanted all of him. No barriers.

Secretly she knew she was safe. Secretly she knew her insides were barren, fallow, and desolate. But he took her so passionately, always as if she was a liquid being, reemerging from the moist fertile soil, fucking like animals, his hands groping her with urgency and need.

Relief pools inside of her and exhilaration electrifies her; the freedom of knowing she has no choice. Yes, it is Dan's baby. She feels it and a woman knows.

And the baby would save them both.

4

There is no recognition in her eyes.

Cliff holds her gaze and his breathing changes to a shallow huff of air, afraid to intrude, afraid not to. She stares at him from her bed as if he is transparent; a ghost. He doesn't want to speak again. He wants her to see him on her own and panic fills him when she doesn't. Finally, Callie blinks and her eyes adjust to his. She's got a blanket over her as if she's chilled.

"Did you—what did you say?"

"I asked you if you got the pictures down." Relief floods his chest and he smiles.

Callie's brow furrows. She begins to shake her head. "Daddy, what are you talking about?"

"I'm talking about Mom's birthday present. You were supposed to get pictures down from the attic—"

Her face darkens. "No—I didn't."

Cliff takes in a deep breath. "Well, I got the picture frame...There's five frames all in one—"

"Who did it? You or Mom."

"Did what?"

Her eyes redden and her chest rises and falls visibly with each breath. "The attic. Who did it?"

Age evaporates from her face like a mist and she's only a child. She's his child and she is lost. Cliff advances past the door jam and stands in the center of her room leaning toward her but his feet seem unwilling to move.

The air is infused with incense, sweet perfume, and a musty undercurrent he can't discern. He clears his throat.

"How about we open a window in here? It's stuffy—"

"Who did it!"

He jumps in spite of himself. "Why are you yelling? I—"

"You are not answering me! I went up to the attic and the carpet is new. Who did it!"

Cliff watches her as her hands wring the blanket into a twisted knot. His mouth opens to answer and his voice fails him. He licks his dry lips.

"She did it, didn't she?" Callie says hoarsely. "She probably couldn't stand the thoughts of her being here even when she's dead. Right? *Right?*"

He almost asks who, but he knows better. Cliff stalks to the window and unlatches it, murmuring to himself. The frame sticks and he uses considerable force to get it open.

"Whew, that's better," he mutters. He inhales, willing the outside air to refresh the room. The influx of air is not fresh and it feels and smells as stale as a mildewed rag. The gauzy drapes entangle him briefly and he fights them away, frantic as if they are cobwebs. When he steps away from the curtains, his daughter's penetrative gaze stops his breath in his chest.

"Why didn't you stop her! She's a selfish, cold-hearted bitch!"

"Hey!" Cliff takes two large steps toward the bed so he towers over Callie. "You will not talk about your mother that way. Do you understand me?"

Callie buries her head for a moment and then raises her eyes to him. "Daddy, I have to tell you something."

Cliff raises his hand protectively before he can stop himself. His hand floats before him in his vision, trembling, and he sees Callie ready herself to tell him more. He has never before struck his child, but he has a fleeting moment when he can think of nothing else that will quash his daughter's words.

"Daddy, there's something you should know...about Mom—"

"I did it."

Her confusion cascades down her face, effectively choking her words back into their proper place. She swallows, her throat convulsing repeatedly, as if she literally ingests his words.

"Your mother had nothing to do with it. I—I did it. I had everything cleaned up…replaced, while you were in the hospital."

Her head shakes before the words even exit her mouth. "No…no—"

"Yes, I did it, Callie. It was me."

Cliff holds his gaze steady with the lie.

Marilyn is on the floor of the attic, sobbing as she rips the stuff up with her bare hands, a sheet covering the soiled stain. Her eyes had been narrowed into angry slits, her voice a growl, siphoning through clenched, angry teeth. They had blamed the dead girl for so long. It's how they survived it.

Cliff's thoughts turn to Chelle and his head jerks back and forth suddenly, as if to dispel unwanted visions. He clamps his eyes shut and his tears are for her, for the loss of her child, for her naked body dripping wet in a cheap hotel while he'd run like a coward.

"How could you?" Callie's voice is barely a whisper.

He sniffs his own emotion back, telling himself he's being brave because he takes the blame for something his wife had done. He tells himself he is brave, but he sees Marilyn's eyes like a rabid animal's and hears their condemnation of the dead girl who almost led their baby, their Callie, to the land of no return and Chelle's naked body drips with water, the blood washed away by his wife. Marilyn tears up the carpet, inch by inch, ripping Chelle at the seams, rending her into so many little pieces, accusing and acrimonious, and all the while, in every instance, he stood afar and aside like the coward he is.

෧෨

"So, what's with all the spooky?"

Ryanne's teeth gleam in the moonlight. "Is it spooky? I thought it was romantic."

"*Candlelight* is romantic. *Abandoned lots* are *not* romantic." Callie steps delicately behind Ryanne and lets out a yelp of pain.

"I told you to wear good shoes. And it's not just *any* abandoned lot."

"And by 'good shoes', I thought you meant Aldos."

"Suburb."

"Shut up. So why the spooky lot?"

"Okay, it may be a little *mysterious*, but it's not *spooky*. I wasn't going for spooky. Even though it is Halloween."

"Halloween is tomorrow night."

"No, tomorrow's Sunday, so Halloween can't be tomorrow night. God negates the Day of the Dead."

Callie stops and almost bumps into the other girl. "You're weird."

Ryanne had stopped to glance around. Seemingly satisfied, she unfurls a foam mat on the ground. "Here, spread this blanket on top of the mat."

Callie glances around at the giant, darkened signs; fractured, skeletal remains of brightly lit denizens awaiting their destiny or doom in the archives of the past.

"I *said* you're weird."

"So you noticed." Ryanne smiles with her eyes as she hands Callie a small plastic cup. "Sit."

Callie obeys, letting another yelp escape her. "Ouch!"

"Careful. There's broken glass everywhere. Stay on the mat." A Burger King sign sits askew on its side, flanked by promises of *Girls, Girls, Girls* and *Dancers of the Desert*, signs that echo the golden days of Vegas.

Ryanne produces two tea candles in glass containers and lights them with a long-tipped lighter. Shadows ebb and flow on her face with the flames and the ink smudge is gone from her cheek. The wind barely touches the encased flames; they flicker, shedding an unexpected warm light on the surrounding exsanguinous, gaunt frames of metal and plastic.

Callie glances around nervously. "Are there rats here? I hate rats."

Ryanne rolls her eyes and pulls a paper bag out of her back pack. She produces a green bottle and a baggy of sugar cubes. She places a water bottle in the center of the mat and gazes hard into Callie's eyes while miniature flames dance in Ryanne's eyes and beckon Callie toward her.

"I've never been here. Can you believe it?" Callie shrugs.

"How could you live here and not visit The Bone Yard?" They both look around as if the dilapidated metal and glass titans hover closer to them than before.

"That's why. 'Cause I live here. It's always here so I take for granted that it'll always be here."

"*That* is a mistake. A thinking error." Ryanne taps her temple. "*Nothing gold can stay.*"

Callie raises her eyes upward and shrinks back. "Oh my God it looks like it's going to step on me."

Ryanne glances up at the giant, red Cinderella shoe adorned with unlit neon bulbs. The underside is almost directly above them, black and ominous. "Look in back of you."

Callie tilts her head backward and exclaims again. "Okay, that's seriously creepy." She turns around partially to see a painted eye of a brunette peeking over a *Showgirls* sign. Her eyes are cocoa brown, the lashes long and wispy.

Ryanne takes a deep breath. "Okay, so here's the thing."

"Uh oh, not 'the thing'."

"Will you hush? Okay, so the last date we went on, you were drunk... you're not tonight, right?"

"Not yet." Callie doesn't tell her about the pills. She doesn't need to know about the pills.

"K, so you were *drunk* and you were all freaked out about your friend, may she rest in p—"

"I don't want to talk about that."

"Hey, this is my deal or whatever, so just lemme finish."

Callie pulls her thin hoodie on her head and pushes her sleeves down over her hands. The wind picks up and dust and particles dance and titter on the still-warm pavement.

"Okay, finish."

"I want tonight to be just about *you* and *me* and...our friendship." Ryanne holds up a clear plastic cup. The liquid inside is opaque white.

"It looks like a cup of clouds." Callie takes it and inhales the scent. "Mmm, licorice."

"It's anise. And it *is* a cup of clouds. See, we're here, among the gods in the clouds…the Gods of Neon."

"Don't forget the Goddesses of Neon." Callie points above her at the giant eye, drinks the concoction and coughs.

"Does it need more water in it?"

Callie shakes her head and shoots the entire cup in a single shot.

A breeze crackles along the ground as if tiny rodents tickle their feet along the gravel. Ryanne makes Callie another drink. She pours the liquor into the glass of water, over sugar cubes on a slotted spoon. Callie's eyes are attached to invisible strings that pull them up. They settle on the giant shoe awaiting its time to pulverize them into the gravel so that they can dance with the scurrying rodents and their dancing feet.

Callie stares at the bottle. "What is it?"

"Absinthe."

Flames shudder and the blanket shifts as the candles' light marks new illuminations on twisted steel. Callie holds another drink and she hums the tune she'd heard on a bad station on her car stereo. It only picks up AM radio. The song asks if 'you know the way to San Jose' and it seems fitting now as she allows Ryanne's mouth to explore her neck and face. She reclines on the mat and the blanket is soft on the back of her legs and head, not like the cinder block at the print shop at all. Their mouths collide and then meld and soon there is no space between either of them, only particles dancing along the gravel and hands, languid and firm, moving over her body.

The wind changes from warm to cool on bare breasts and then hot when Ryanne's breasts press up to hers, almost sticky. Nipples erect against moisture against warm winds against hands tugging insistently on cut-offs and a brunette with a painted brown eye and a lost slipper who smells of lilies watches furtively between gasps and undulating hips. Hands rake through soft hair, fine and smooth, tickling her fingertips, licking at the very tip of her and the brunette head nods in acquiescence as the omniscient brown eye winks and blesses the union. Callie thanks her for finally releasing her to another. Tears pool in her ears, but her mouth is dry and her eyes are closed. Callie reaches and finds the plastic cup, sits up slightly, and Ryanne watches Callie from below her belly as Callie thirstily downs the next cup of ghostly clouds.

∽

The son of a bitch is too heavy.

Dan pushes again, but the washing machine won't budge. It's filled with water and saturated clothes and the noise it made before the agitating ceased was foreboding. He shoves again, and leans over to see the hoses, like a gnarled nest of snakes covered in fine, gray dust. One last heave and the snap in his back coincides with the minute movement of the machine.

"Goddamnit! *Mother* fucker…*fuck*." He gingerly sinks onto his right knee, his upper body frozen in place like a Greek statue of a discus thrower.

"Ooohh—kay. Easy." His other knee comes down too hard and he winces with a line of unintelligible obscenities.

"Great, just *great*." On both knees, he attempts to stand but his back seizes and he sinks his forehead against the metal washing machine door. The icy metal clears his head.

Breathe through it.

As the spasm ebbs, he sinks all the way to the floor and allows his shoulder to rest on the chilly linoleum of the laundry room. He holds his head inches from the floor, immobile.

"Never learns. He never learns to call the fucking plumber…nice going, genius." Dan's voice ricochets off the metal and his head finally rests all the way down onto the tile as a breath heaves out of him. "Okay…just relax. Just a flesh wound."

He knows the more tense he is, the longer the spasm takes to diminish. He ignores the awkward angle of his body on the tile and takes in deep breaths, allowing his shoulders to become heavier and heavier. He closes his eyes and breathes.

Like a drain, the pain circles the ruined disk in his spine, and the radius shrinks with each calibrated breath. His eyes remain closed but then they open and stare underneath the washer.

A gray mottled form, like a rag, sits near the back. It must have been placed under the washing machine's corner to stop the ceaseless off-balance clanging that occurs with each load. Dan's valiant shove had set it free and now, curious and with a sinking feeling in his gut, he reaches for it, grimacing with the effort.

The item is a sock, and the miniature argyle design lining the top is unmistakable. He used to do the laundry. Breathing steady but shallowly, he pulls it toward him and stares at it, noting the gray lint, like a mist, covering the once-white material. The sob comes out of nowhere, jagged and harsh, and he forces himself to sit upright through his pain.

He places his forehead on his knees and weeps, great heaving breathes punctuating the ragged sobs. Before that moment he had been sure the wound was healing, sure he had moved past it. But the gash is fresh, gushing, like a sucking chest wound, with only a gray, mottled sock to staunch it.

He tries to stand, but his back protests with another spasm. Awkwardly, he grasps the side of the washing machine, sock enclosed in his fist, and stands with a guttural shout of pain from deep inside.

Finally on his feet, he tries to catch his breath, his face soaked with tears. He doesn't wipe his sleeve across his cheeks. He doesn't care if his wife sees him like this again, like so many times before. He wonders if seeing him will jog that seemingly absent maternal woman he'd married and she would wail with him like an Old World widow, wearing black and calling out for release from grief.

Dan makes his way up to the kitchen, then up the short flight of stairs to the office, the room that was once his daughter's. He walks in and a filmy milieu stretches in front of his gaze like a blanket covering the room. He can see her bed still, see her posters lining the walls. He can see the mosquito net she insisted on having over her bed. He can almost smell her perfume, like cotton candy mingled with lilies, and he can see her brown eyes greeting him before her dimples deepen into a smile.

The only thing left of her in this room is the bureau, cleaned out of all of her belongings. He staggers over to it, his weeping overcoming him, and opens the top drawer, now the home of hand towels and wash cloths. He smells the gray sock, and the dust tickles his nose, so he slaps it fiercely against his leg. He begs for the sock to be unwashed, so that any part of her can be with him as he inhales, but it smells like lavender soap and old water.

He opens the bureau drawer wider and places the sock lovingly in the very back. Through his tears he smiles and whispers, "You can stay here. You can stay right here at home."

෴

Marilyn's water glass is replenished again and she doesn't know why she's so thirsty. *Dehydration*, she thinks.

The restaurant is noisy but surprisingly empty, the brunch crowd preferring to sit outside on a rare late morning respite from the sweltering heat. It's the place Dan and she met before the first time they'd slept together, after a long day at The Center. She blushes at her bathetic notion, but she has been feeling positively *gushy* all week. Dan hasn't called her back—he knows not to call her back. But she'd left a message and knew he'd be there shortly.

She practices what she will say. Mid-practice, however, the server comes and harangues her to order an appetizer, or the busboy fills her glass or someone catches eye and she looks away, sure they know her from somewhere.

Dan, I know I said it was over, but I think it's just beginning—

"Ma'am, would you like to start out with a drink?"

Marilyn's head snaps up. "No, thank you. Just water for now."

"We have raspberry lemonade, freshly—"

"I can't—just water. Thank you."

The server smiles and walks away, reluctant to leave without an order and Marilyn's stomach lurches with the tell-tale stab of pain from an empty, dry-heaved stomach.

It's a boy.

She muses and tells herself the tale one more time—how does she know its Dan's baby? He'll ask her that.

Babies know when two people love each other—babies know and they come to them and I don't love Cliff anymore and it's been too long—

"Have you been helped?"

"What? Oh, yes, I'm fine."

"Can I get you started with an appetizer? We have artichoke stuffed—"

"I'm waiting for someone."

"Okay, I'll check back in a bit."

Marilyn's stomach cringes as her mind involuntarily goes to food. The smell in the cafe twists her insides in two. She remembers sharing a turtle cheesecake with Dan at that very table before he'd ravaged her in the motel. She shifts in her chair at the sudden tingling warmth that pools between her legs.

Do you remember the first night, when you laid me on the bed and gently spread my knees apart? You buried your—

"More water?" The busboy's towel-wrapped pitcher hovers near her empty water glass.

"Yes, please, thank you."

She ignores the urge to run to the bathroom. She pulls her napkin up to her nose to quell the smell of freshly sizzled shrimp fajitas. Perhaps some bread.

I know this is crazy, but a woman knows, and I think—I'm going to—we're going to have a son.

Marilyn's heart rams unmercifully against her ribs and her hand, trembling, rises up as the server catches her eye.

"Yes, ma'am, are you ready—"

"Bread? Please…thank you."

What I'm saying Dan, is I—I want you. I know we said we wouldn't let it get that far, but I did and I do and I choose you—

The bread is covered by a white napkin and the steam rises out of the sides. The odor causes her gut to double over inside of her and she winces. Her hand feels for the warm, spongy loaf and her mouth is dry again.

I'm sicker now because I'm older, or it could be a boy. It's probably a boy.

She drinks the water and sees the two pink lines unmistakable on the test, and even clearer on the second test, and she should have brought them to prove it to him, make it real, but they are covered in pee.

"Still waiting?"

Marilyn looks at her phone. No calls, she's waited 45 minutes. He would never be that late. Would he?

"Yes, thank you."

She tries to focus on the menu, and she drinks more ice water to wash down the bread, which sits like a fetid lump in her belly. The other server approaches and the door opens at the front of the cafe and a gaggle of women, chirping and chattering, waft in with a collective cloud of perfume and bodies.

"Where are your restrooms?"

The server points the way as Marilyn scoots her chair back, bumping it into the table in back of her. No one is there so there's no one to apologize to as she strides to the back, to the barely-lit restroom, colored in oranges and bronze and gold. She kneels on the cement floor and watches her water break from her mouth into the toilet below.

ༀ

"Who's calling you, Dan? I swear to God, don't people leave messages anymore?"

"Unknown number. Probably that wrong number again from last Spring. You remember that guy? Jesus. Even after I told him it was wrong, he kept calling."

"Well, he was old, remember?" Chelle smiles and nudges him. "Thank you for making the salad. Your back feeling better?"

"Yes, and you're welcome." He nudges her back and they both smile, but his face is stiff. His phone jumps off the counter as it vibrates again and Chelle glances at him, eyebrow raised. Dan turns the phone off. "Problem solved."

She has lost her place in the recipe book; the words blur in front of her. Dan's rhythmic chopping punctuates the silent room.

Chop, chop, chop.

"You didn't even look." Her face turns toward him. She can't be this paranoid, and she can't bring it up again. It's unspoken, like a line in sand, with errant particles and grains tumbling to and fro, unnoticed. "It might have been someone you know."

"Doubt it."

"But how do you *know*?"

"I don't. Does it matter?" He nudges her with his hip again. His smile deepens. "I'm where I wanna be. If it's work, they can kiss my ass. It's my afternoon off."

"And if it's Andy? He's not your friend right now."

"He can handle whatever cluster fuck is going on without me. He's my supervisor for a reason. Stop worrying. What's the cilantro for?"

"The recipe." Shadows settle over her mind and she wants to drop it but she can't. The worry niggles at her brain and she thinks of any excuse to continue the line of conversation.

"So, let me see your phone then, if you're so sure it's not Andy."

Dan doesn't pause his chopping. "I hate cilantro. Can't it go without it?"

She rolls her eyes in exasperation. "No, it's *baked cilantro*! Now let me see…"

"Baked cilantro? You let *me* see—" He reaches for her recipe book and with a quick swipe of his hand, he snags his phone and drops it in his pocket. "It's Thai Chicken—cilantro is *optional*. You know I hate cilantro…"

Chelle tries to grab the book from him, smiling as he attempts to tickle her. "I'm not ticklish, Dan."

"I know, and I hate that about you." As he moves toward her, her hand reaches down for his pocket. He bars her from it and attempts to tickle her further.

"Ow! Now you're just poking me." He grabs her around the waist to go in for a kiss. She pushes him away too harshly and her hands stay poised in mid-air. Her face is flushed. "Why won't you let me see your phone?"

He gives her a bewildered look and her face darkens.

"Chelle, c'mon. Don't do this. You know you're just being paranoid."

"No, I don't know I'm being paranoid. I need a *trust baseline*, Dan."

"A trust *what?*"

"I have to see if you're being honest with me. Prove it and then I can go on faith after that."

"What are you talking about? Honey, c'mon…kiss me."

"I don't think it's too much to ask. Just let me see who's been calling you."

He searches her face and reaches in his pocket.

"Fine! *Jesus!*"

Her stomach unfurls slightly as he hands her the phone. She glances up at his face. His eyes are slits, staring off to the side like a kid being asked to give up his stolen cigarettes. She berates herself silently.

"I'm sorry. I—you're right. I don't want to look at it."

"How about you look at it and I'll look at yours."

Dan's face has hardened and her hands flutter up to her chest. "I said I was sorry, Dan. You're right. We need to—"

"So you're saying I can't see *your* phone, now."

"I'm saying we could go crazy living like this—"

"Bullshit. You don't like the tit-for-tat. Who you been talking to? Anyone I know?"

"No one!" Tears brim in her eyes while her phone sits flashing on the table next to the garage door. Cliff's number is in it, along with his name. There was a time when part of her wanted Dan to find it. She doesn't know why she hasn't removed it.

"Well, let's go and see, shall we?" Dan's face sports a fierce grin. It is not all malice, but much of it is, and she lunges for his arm.

"Dan!"

"What? I'm just checking—"

"Goddamnit, stop it!" She stands in front of him, eyes red, chest heaving.

All of the teasing drains from his eyes. "What the fuck, Chelle? What don't you want me to see?"

Pin-prickly sensation causes her upper lip to swell with her tears. "N—nothing. Nothing." Her whisper is so soft, he leans in to listen. "You just have to trust me."

Dan's face is pale and stark with suspicion. "Like...like *you* trust *me*."

"Yes. Like I trust you." She nods her head and moves toward him, wrapping her arms around his shoulders. She nestles her head against him and moves toward his ear. "I'm sorry."

Dan's arms encircle her waist and he murmurs into her hair. "Me, too."

5

Ryanne tickles Callie's nose with a strand of her hair. Callie's eyes remain closed but she smiles and lazily waves her hand.

"Will you *stop?*" She opens her eyes and Ryanne's face breaks into a grin.

"*Sleepy.*"

"You kept me out late." Callie reaches up with both arms and yawns. She opens her eyes and surveys the tiny bedroom, hung with drying clothes and black and white photos. "I don't remember even coming here."

"Oh great, thanks."

"I remember *being* here, jeez."

Ryanne pulls her close and the warmth of her skin causes Callie's to warm and shiver all at once.

"You know," Ryanne says, "I don't bring just anyone to the Bone Yard and then my place."

Callie's eyes focus and take in the other girl's gray-blue eyes. Darkened smudges of mascara and eyeliner frame them and the effect is stunning. Callie kisses her and the silence encloses them like a blanket. When they part, Callie stares at her tattoo on her chest, the intricate details mesmerizing her. A slight pulsation of pain begins behind her eyes. She needs water. And pills.

"So what does it mean?" Callie traces her finger lightly over Ryanne's chest tattoo.

Ryanne bows her head and props herself on her elbow. "The roses are for me, 'cause no one ever gave me any."

"And this—the grenade with wings thingy? Kind of…explosive."

"It's because when I love, someone always pulls the pin out."

"Messy."

"*Or* overwhelming and yummy." Ryanne's eyes shine. "Have you ever loved someone so much you felt like your heart would explode?"

A heavy weight infuses Callie's body. She lies back on the pillow and watches the ceiling, plastered with bird posters surrounding the over-head light. She takes even breaths and wills the image of the past night away from her. But she sees the Bone Yard, the sand, the brown, neon eye hovering in Marin's face; she sees neon tears trickling down, dangerous and explosive.

"I don't know. I mean, yeah—"

"Which is it?"

"Yeah." The weight in her body moves and centers around her chest and she can't breathe. The sensation is almost pleasant; she welcomes the heavy drape, too tired to move it away. "Yeah."

"Was it *her?*"

Callie watches the birds, static on the posters, yet in mid-flight. She wonders if they were ever free. Callie fights for control of her lips, but they tremble and soon the tears pool in her eyes and slide down her temples into her hair.

Ryanne nestles into the pillow next to her and brushes her arm with a kiss. "What happened?"

Callie shakes her head, her hair tangling behind her on the pillow.

"You can tell me, Callie."

Her head continues to shake as the tears burn fresh in her eyes and her nose tingles. "I can't…"

Ryanne pulls her closer. "It's okay. I'm here."

"Not for long."

Callie's mind races through her purse, searching with her mind if she has some pills left. She needs one now more than ever.

"Whatever. You don't scare me and I'm not going anywhere."

Callie's laugh is mirthless. She brings her arm up to wipe her face. "You don't even know me."

"But I wanna know you." Ryanne brushes Callie's hair from her forehead and the gesture conjures a barrage of images: scary dreams, fevered nights, cold hospital rooms with blinking lights. Her mother's hand, so soft and now so cold. Callie's mouth opens slightly to allow a soundless sob escape her.

"I'm sorry, Callie. I'm sorry I made you sad." Callie's forearms move over her face like shutters. "Look, Suburb, I've seen worse meltdowns than this, okay? You can cry all you want I'm not going to—"

"I did it." Callie can't stop now, and the silence she'd held burns—an antechamber with flames licking her insides. "Oh, *God*!"

"No you didn't, c'mon..."

"Yes! I *did*!"

Ryanne's soothing movement stops and her brows knit as she frowns. "Callie, what...are you talking about?"

Callie's arms move down to her sides, then cross over her chest as if she lay in an open casket. Her whole body quakes. Her nose runs with her eyes and she doesn't move to wipe them. She's naked.

"I gave her the pills."

"She... killed herself?"

"*I did it*! I gave—"

"You didn't make her swallow!" Ryanne has her wrist and she holds tight.

"You don't understand." Callie's whisper is strained. "I've never told anyone about it."

"Why did you give her the pills?"

"To help! I only wanted to help. But—but she...she was gone so fast! So I took the rest—"

"You took pills, too." Ryanne's eyes search Callie's face and she nods, a new wave of sobs spilling over her. "She didn't want to die and...you did." Ryanne's eyes redden as she strokes Callie's forehead.

"Everyone thought...you know? I mean, everyone thought...but it wasn't a pact," Callie opens her eyes; a deluge of tears wet her cheeks as pain graces her features. "It was a murder."

᪥

She'll hate it.

A veritable eyesore, she'll say.

Nothing about it is neutral, and Marilyn likes neutral. Everything she wears, everything they own, is brown and beige and white. Only she calls them 'camel', 'taupe' and 'cocoa'. It's *their* house, not just *her* house and he has a *right*.

A man's home is his castle.

He'd neglected going to art galleries because he didn't like going alone. Marilyn hated the art he loved. She liked her wall art to *blend*.

He'd met a woman here at the City Lights Gallery once, a few years back. He suspected she was there to meet someone like him—someone with cash and a ring. A professional mistress. She'd played him, and he almost took the bait. But what kind of guy fucks around on his wife while she's in the hospital with cancer? He didn't do it—couldn't bring himself to do it. She'd even offered—in a very indirect way, to suck him off in his car. She probably thought his "wife with cancer" story was a ploy. She had acted all concerned. Wondered if he needed comfort. What he'd needed was some balls. Cliff remembers her blond hair and the cherry red lips, wavy hair a la Jean Harlow, or like that chick in "Gilda"…Rita Hayworth, wasn't it? He chews his lips and thinks about the woman, now amalgamated with Rita Hayworth. The lips and golden hair, her face blemishless, her body that of Rita's in a long, sequined dress. He thinks about how he'd let any chump Marilyn wanted in her pants, but he couldn't fuck a clear and present whore.

"Stunning, isn't it?"

Startled out of his reverie, he looks to his left and down. The gallery employee stands at his elbow like an old friend, a comrade.

"It is quite nice."

'Nice?' Salads are nice. Old women are nice. Jesus, what the hell?

"It's so vibrant. Notice the way her arm is portrayed as moving using the background. You can almost hear her playing."

The dark-haired woman in the panting plays the cello. The point of view is from behind; her bare back as taut as her bow as it's raised to strike the strings. The woman's head is bowed, and Cliff feels he lurks close to her as she plays. The background is indeed alive, swirling with motion, as if the woman plays a concerto just for him. Her dark, unruly hair stirs him, and he thinks of Chelle in the only way his mind will let him, eyes half-closed, mouth parted.

"The artist uses a rhythm of color here that is similar to a fifth, which is fascinating because the cello is tuned in perfect fifths."

His mouth is open slightly and saliva pools under his tongue. He can almost smell her. His breath quickens.

"How much?"

The gallery worker smiles. "Let me go check for you."

He watches her walk away; a tiny, wide woman with sensible heels. Her ass, though, it curves like Chelle's ass.

The colors collide in a symphony of sound—reds and teals, golds and indigos. Green, violet, *alive*. Nothing neutral, nothing taupe.

The woman returns, still smiling. She's Asian, with plump cheeks and friendly eyes enlarged by spectacles. "Ten-fifty."

"I'll give you nine-hundred."

Her smile's light is doused a little. "I'm not sure—"

"Look," he turns his full body toward her, his cock almost turgid from thinking of Chelle. He suddenly wants her to see it, to look down and see his cock protruding like a flag, a weapon. Something with which to reckon. "Artists have day jobs unless they're *that* good. You call the artist and tell her—"

"—*Him*. It's—he's a—a man—"

"Good. You tell him, right now, you have someone who's willing to slap nine-hundred dollars down on his art. In cash. Can you do that for me?"

"I suppose I can call…"

"You do that. I've got a few minutes."

The gallery employee's gait turns authoritative at once as she heads toward the offices.

Marilyn will hate it.

Just like I hate it when I know she's seeing some asshole on the side. Just like I have to take her after. What's good for the goose is good for the gander. She'll fucking hate it.

The low sound of a cello hums through him, pulsing blood through his veins, through his body, giving his cock life. He reaches down and adjusts and sees Chelle's naked back to him, black curls cascading down. He comes behind her, and the dead daughter is no longer a ghost to haunt him, no longer spectator, but a wisp of music playing far away, playing well away from him, his life, his world. They are all safe, Callie is safe, and Chelle, she is just a woman, and she needs him. She needs him to shoot life into her, juice into her; she needs to feel alive. But there is more: He needs to fuck the woman because her man had fucked his. It is primordial, it is savage, and it's in his cock.

He's at half-mast when the gallery worker returns and he doesn't care. He remains facing the painting, its colors coursing through his vision, pumping his blood throughout him.

"The artist agreed to nine—"

"Of course he did." Cliff turns to her, a half-smile on his lips. "It's a beautiful piece and I knew it was mine."

"So it's for you. I thought maybe it was a gift."

"It is a gift. It's a gift for my wife."

"Oh, I'm sure she'll love it."

Cliff's smile widens and he looks the woman directly in the eyes. "It will take her breath away."

∞

She has a time between her nap and eating lunch where she feels almost human. Marilyn's cheeks are rosy from the arid heat of the late morning, and her throat is parched even though she's guzzling water. She knows the inevitable task of lunch will come, along with the inevitable visit to the bathroom. It's ten a.m. She'll only stay till lunch.

Marilyn scans the parking lot one more time; Dan isn't there. She doesn't know if he even comes to The Center anymore. She relaxes her tense shoulders and exits her car. She doesn't want to hear his excuses, his whining about being trapped—trapped doing what? She hasn't spoken to him in weeks but he couldn't be back at home...

A familiar pain sizzles through her insides.

The Center's door closes behind her as she walks to the front counter.

Stacey, the crisis worker who never seems to leave, sits at the front.

"Hi, Marilyn."

She smiles and can't quite get it to reach her eyes. "Hi."

"You look tired."

"That's an understatement."

"Allen will be in at noon, why don't you go home and get some rest?"

"I'll be okay."

"You need to eat, girl. You've lost weight."

Marilyn's stomach lurches painfully and unconsciously she places her hand over her abdomen. "No food."

Stacey's eyes widen. "Are you...?"

Marilyn thinks hard about her answer. What could possibly happen if Dan found out this way? He might seek *her* out. Marilyn shrugs and raises her eyebrows.

"Oh my God! Congratulations!"

"No one knows, so—"

"Oh, I won't say anything—" then the question flits across her face like a red time-stamp. Stacey picks up a folder, suddenly harried.

"Well, okay, it's been pretty quiet today, b—"

Before she can finish the front door bell chimes. Marilyn recognizes the man who enters, but can't place him.

"Can we help you?"

The man smiles to reveal bright teeth, almost too bright under the fluorescent lightning. "Marilyn? It's me Dave..."

"Oh, God...*Dave*." Marilyn laughs, embarrassed. She leans on the counter for support. "I'm sorry, I'm not feeling so hot today and my brain's gone back to bed."

"Well, you look terrific. In person."

She and Dave had been chatting it up on Facebook for weeks. His showing up here is surprising; he hadn't indicated he'd be dropping by. "Thanks, you too. Is there something you need here?"

"Well, yeah. Can you take a walk?"

Outside, she takes in a deep breath but the air is heavy in her chest and quickly fills her stomach uneasily. "Whew, it's gotten hot."

"Yeah, it usually lets up by now, huh?"

"So what brings you to the Youth Suicide Prevention Center—I can only hope it's nothing personal."

"Well, yes—and no. You remember Rory DeSoto? From high school?"

"Yeah…I remember Rory."

"Her son just killed himself last week."

"Oh God, no."

"I know. He was only twenty-two."

"Oh my God, that's so awful."

"And it got me thinking about the work you do here."

Marilyn wracks her brain for Dave's line of work. She remembers being mildly impressed. He had been a nobody in high school. Of course, she had been with Cliff back then.

"And what were you thinking?"

"You remember I'm the producer for My News 4. This is the kind of thing that needs to get out there—on a large scale, Marilyn."

Her mouth is dry and she licks her lips. "I'm not the person to talk to—"

"But you are," Dave moves closer to her and the smell of his cologne is actually soothing. Grapefruit and sandalwood. "Because I read the story on you and your daughter."

Her spine stiffens immediately. Before she can speak, her legs waver under her like a mirage and she pitches forward slightly. Dave wraps his massive arms around her and holds on, steadying her.

"I need to get out of the heat."

"I'm sorry, honey, let's get you inside and get you some water."

When they enter the cool foyer, Marilyn collapses in a chair near the doors in the waiting room. Dave walks back to the cooler and brings her a tiny white cone of ice water.

"Thanks…" she takes a very small sip and lays her head back on the wall.

"Marilyn, I know Ellie, the woman who did your story—"

"That bitch made our lives a living hell—*for her story*."

"She was young, new, she had a lot to learn, don't be too harsh, Marilyn. Ultimately her goal was to help people, warn them—"

"Her goal was to get on the front page, and she did. I had to pull my daughter out of school, take her to counselors, hide from neighbors—we almost moved!"

"We would be much more tasteful—"

"You want to do a news show about *us*?"

"No, no, no, about The Center, here. It would help if you and your family would be willing to talk to us—"

"Well, we aren't. I agree that doing something on The Center is a good idea, but leave us out of it, please..."

"Okay, okay, I can do that." His arm circles around her and she is protected by it, by the scent of sandalwood and a warm, meaty arm and his clean shave, his handsome face. "Shh, it's alright."

Marilyn realizes tears are running down her face. He grabs a box of tissue on one of the tables and holds it in front of her. She sniffs. "I'm sorry—it was such a horrible time—"

"Oh, God, I can only imagine. I'm sorry I dredged it up for you."

She wipes her nose and closes her eyes, willing the aching in her head to subside.

"Marilyn, let me take you to dinner tonight. Please? I'd really like your input and I swear to you, your family will be protected from this. But your insight would be invaluable."

His scent covers her and her nausea is held at bay by the warmth spreading through her, and she moves her shoulder against his chest while burying her head deeper into it.

"*No* Mexican."

He laughs and squeezes around her shoulders. "You got it."

෮

"I want you to know I'm in deep *like*."

"What in the hell does that mean?" Callie coughs and hands the joint to Ryanne. The pot has helped her forget the horror that had just played back in her mind.

"That means," Ryanne inhales and holds her breath, smiling, "I haven't waked n' baked since I was sixteen."

"So you're in deep *like*, huh?" Callie lounges back onto the pillow, holding her hands above her head.

Ryanne blushes at the suggestive pose and crawls up Callie's body, kissing her belly. "Yeah...*deep*." Callie places her hand on Ryanne's head as she works her way up to her chin, and finally her lips. "But I can't love you... *yet*."

Callie searches Ryanne's face. "Oh yeah? *Yet*...what does that even mean?"

"It means *yet*."

"Because of what I said, you're thinking I'm all psycho now, right?"

"No." Ryanne's face is blank, but her eyes move back and forth on Callie's face. "I just wish you'd talk to me."

"And tell you what? How I killed my friend?"

"Don't say that, it's not funny."

Callie stifles a smile, the pot making her giddy. "Don't worry, I won't hurt you."

Ryanne shakes her head. "It's not me I worry about, Suburb."

"Oh God..."

"Yeah, right, because you're *so careful* with yourself."

"I wear my seatbelt." Callie breaks into a giggle and Ryanne's face hardens.

"You think this is funny? 'Cause this is why I say *I can't* yet. Because you've got this weird death wish—"

"I do not!"

"Like fucking *hell* you don't! Why should I invest my emotions and heart into someone who wants to just crash into a brick wall? Huh?"

Callie is silent, her face and stomach dropping like a piece of freight. "I don't want...that."

"You act like you do."

Callie's gaze moves from Ryanne's face to just behind her shoulder. Her vision blurs and her head feels so heavy, like she could just fall to the side and sleep without dreams.

"She's always with me." Callie's voice is a whisper and her lips are numb. Her eyes move to the soft light at the window.

"What do you mean? Your friend?"

Callie nods slowly. "It's my punishment for not being good enough, not being brave enough."

"That's not true. It's not true. You were saved for a reason—"

"And Marin had no purpose?"

"No, no, I'm not saying—look, what I mean is you can do good things with your life and help people. You don't have to turn it all into pain."

Callie's breathing deepens; she speaks and moves as if in a trance. "But that's all there is. Day, night, whatever. She isn't even Marin to me anymore. She's just pain. And I feel her hovering near me every second of every day and I don't know how to tell her to leave. She won't leave!" Tears spring to her eyes again and her chin reddens and crumples. The pot dulls her insides, but the pain has a life all its own.

Ryanne wraps her arms around Callie, "Shh... listen, it's *you* keeping her here, not the other way around. She's at peace. You're not, and you keep her alive in here." She touches Callie's chest.

"I promised her I'd keep her there...I promised her..." Her voice cracks with sobs and she falls to the side.

"You've fulfilled it, Callie, you have. It's time to let her go."

"I can't. I still see her and smell her and want her—I can't just forget! I love her! And she *is* there, I'm telling you..."

Ryanne holds her quaking body, kissing her hair. "What if we ask her what she wants?"

Callie raises her tear stained face. "What?"

"I mean it. No fucking around. We ask her what she wants. Does she want you to keep suffering or does she want you to move on? We'll ask her."

"I don't believe in that shit." Callie's eyes show more white than before and her shuddering causes her to wrap the blanket near her breasts.

"You don't have to believe in anything. Look…" Ryanne stands up and walks over to the dresser. She's wearing boxers and no bra and Callie stares at her smooth skin and wants to suddenly feel it on her all over again, like a warm, velvet blanket, keeping her safe.

Ryanne brings over a magnifying glass and a magazine and plops down on the bed. "Okay, we—oh wait…" She jumps up and grabs two tea candles and her lighter. She lights them and places them on the nightstand and then flips off the light. The effect is marred by the morning light streaming past the bed sheet curtain over the window. The air around Callie feels colder suddenly and she pulls the blanket up around her shoulders. Ryanne opens the side table drawer and pulls out a pen and a notebook.

"This is my journal. I've written about you a lot, actually—"

"What are you doing?"

Ryanne's face is stony. "We're going to ask."

"Come on, it's not funny—"

"I'm not trying to be funny."

"Then it's not cool, whatever it is you're doing."

"What's her name. I can't remember."

"No, I'm not going to—"

"Do you want to be free or not! What's her name?"

"Marin! God, her name is—was, Marin." Callie's hands scrunch the sheet under her chin, her eyes wide and fearful.

Ryanne opens the magazine to a long article and places the magnifying glass over it. She sits silently, her hands lightly touching the glass and Callie only stares at it, wonder and fear gracing her face. Ryanne closes her eyes and moves the glass around on the page. The crackling sound unnerves Callie and she closes her eyes, too, sniffing into the sheet.

She hears Ryanne scratching with her pen, hears the magazine crinkle as if Marin is there, clawing her way up through the pages. Callie throws her hands over her ears but the sound is deafening. She feels the bed move and for an instant, she hears screaming and realizes it's her own.

"Callie, stop!"

"*I can't do this!*"

"It's done! I wrote down all the words the glass showed me! See?"

Callie sees words scribbled on the page and she can't make them out so she peers closer.

Ryanne snaps up the book and clears her throat. "The message says, "Allow me to sleep.""

Callie's lips tremble and she shakes her head. "No. It—it said more than that."

Ryanne frowns slightly. "Oh, she also says remember to moisturize."

Callie stares at her, waiting for the smile to come, but Ryanne's face remains frozen in a stony stare.

"You are such a bitch." Callie tastes bile in her throat.

"Callie, I *am not,* I—"

"I wasn't talking to you."

6

The hair straightener only flattens her curls momentarily. With each layer the waves return. *Pubic head.* Her unfortunate nickname in school. Chelle spritzes the section of her head with hair spray, willing it to stay. She looks more dignified with straight hair. Refined. Or maybe she doesn't want to be such a stark contrast to *her.*

Whore.

Marilyn had been Dan's mysterious caller. And he knew it. Chelle knew he'd had new messages; now he doesn't. Dan had kept the messages, and she realizes nothing is over between the lovers.

She is such a fool.

And she hasn't heard from Cliff since he bolted from the hotel. Why should she expect any different? Both men love *her.* She looks like she'd be a stone slab in bed; an icy cockpit. But that's what they want, isn't it? Women who play hard to get; women who say "no" and play demure and tease. They don't want willing women who say "I want to fuck"; who sweat, and smell heady and musky, who are fertile and round. The fucking men— *her men*, they want a stick woman with her red hair and her frail frame and her white skin and straight, silken hair neatly done. Dignified. Controlled.

I can be dignified. I can have control.

She powders her face so the naturally dewy shine of her skin is muted. It lightens it slightly. Her ethnicity lies in her eyebrows, too—dark and thick. She wants to pluck, but she's afraid she'd look like her mother who had to draw them on at the end. Chelle's lips are full. *Her lips are thin.* Precise. How a man must feel—how *powerful* he must feel to cover her small, thin lips with his large, sweltering mouth, hungry and hot for a pale, frail, piece of ass.

"Shit!" Her mascara smudges on her lower lid because her hand shakes. Sweat already graces her upper lip. She waves at her face to cool it. Today is her half-day at work, and usually they wear business casual, but today she wears a skirt. She needs to look a certain way today, needs to turn a head, maybe three, so she knows she's not dead—or worse, invisible.

As suspected, her hair cascades in waves, defying even the hair spray and iron. She combs it smooth and sprays again. She presses matte lipstick to her lower lip. The color is a dark mauve, enticing the natural hue of her cheeks to appear. The matte downplays her lips, makes them less full. *Less. Always less.*

She would have to drop thirty pounds to look like *her*. She'd have to be pale with straight, strawberry tresses and fine bone structure to look like *her*. And she would have to be weak.

She's seen her. At the funeral. Once pumping gas. Once walking in the mall. She looks as though an angry wind would blow her down. Her porcelain skin and carefully arched, strawberry eyebrows...*whore*. Her narrow, up-turned nose.

Chelle gazes into the mirror, nostrils flaring, knuckles white from holding to the edge of the counter. Her mascara is in danger of smearing as trembling lips and angry tears threaten. She brings a finger up and staunches the tear at the corner of her eye. She traces the bridge of her nose, marveling at its width. Everything is exaggerated, nothing delicate. Nothing precise.

Of course they want the porcelain doll and not the peasant woman who gets her hands dirty in the fields. *Of course.*

She has her mother's peasant hands: long, chunky fingers, short nails. No taper at the end. Long and stubby all at once. Her mother's hands worked in the fields as a child and formed around beans and corn and weeds. They formed and traveled through her genes to Chelle, even though her office work doesn't get the dirt under her nails. Only ink and paper cuts, thin as a hairline fissure; the only thing thin on her large frame.

As she gazes into the mirror she sees her bra is no longer pure white. It has grown dingy with wear, and suddenly her chest breaks out in red blotches. As her face crumples, her heavy breasts undulate with her labored breathing. *Of course.* Tears no longer threaten, but come in a flash flood; in a glimmer of movement, her brush sails across the bathroom, clattering into the bathtub. She tears her bra from her body and it follows the brush. Her hair cinches up into deeper waves and her lipstick smears on her hand as she wipes at her mouth. The towel bar digs into her back as she leans against it, wiping at her eyes.

Finally, she rummages through her lingerie drawer, a box, really, a canvas box on the floor of her closet, and finds her black bra. It's lacy and shows her nipples through the material. She doesn't wear it often; Dan prefers small nipples and hers are large and round and dark. *Her* nipples are probably tiny, pale, pink…flat…unresponsive. *Cunt, whore.* Chelle wipes at her face.

She puts on her bra and the lace is rough against the nubby flesh. She searches in her closet for a dark silk blouse to wear with her skirt. Today she would wear black and revel in being a peasant and Latina and a woman in her prime, even though the two men in her life want a vapid, pale facsimile of her dark beauty. She wipes off her powder and tends to her eyes.

The silken blouse is cool and soft against her skin; the material cools her body so her breaths take a slow, even rhythm. She reapplies her lipstick and blots her face, flushed now, and rosy as if from a heated union.

Dan works late tonight—until three a.m.. Is that really his schedule? Does she have to start checking up on him all over again? No, she can't—she won't.

She smoothes her hair down and smiles, willing her tears at bay. Cliff will have no choice but to deal with her today. No more running, no more evading. She is not naked in the shower, dripping wet. He will have nowhere to go, and soon, neither will Dan.

⁊৹

She *knows* he works the late shift. She *knows* he needs to sleep and she does everything as loud as she possibly can. Dan places another pillow over his head but she's now talking to herself—*out loud.*

"Jesus fucking Christ, Chelle, can you keep it down?"

"What did you say to me?"

He sits up on his elbows, eyes bleary. "Why are you being as loud as possible, huh? I gotta sleep."

"So you just scream at me like the dog?"

"No, the dog doesn't try to wake me up."

She huffs out a breath, eyes blazing. But that won't be the end of her. She storms out and then, as he knew she would, re-enters the room. "Ya know, it'd be nice if you noticed how I *looked* for a change."

Dan has his arm across his eyes. "You look mad."

"You're hilarious. You know that? No, you're a *joke*."

Dan's breath deepens and his chest lights, burning him from inside. He sits up and yanks the covers off himself. "Okay, I'll bite, why am I a joke?"

She stands and stares at him, words seeming to broil up and out of her. "You live a lie. You're not the man I fell in love with—the man with a *conscience* and *morals*!"

"Oh, I'm no longer Catholic, so I don't have any morals—" He wants to take it back but he can't. He'd stepped right into it.

"You still love *her* and you share my bed. Is that moral to you?"

His indignation erupts. "I share your bed out of *choice*, not because I *have* no choice!"

"Oh please. You broke it off with *her*? Is that it? If she crooked her finger, you'd come running. At least your Catholic guilt made you a man!"

"Why are you so fucking concerned with my religion, my—my former religion? A religion you abandoned a long time ago? Huh?"

She stalks over to him. Her voice is quiet. "Because at least when you were practicing, you knew who you were. Now, you're just some pair of *lying pants* in my bed."

"If that's all I am to you, why did you take me back?"

Both of their voices are low, now—whispers. "Because I felt *sorry* for you. I *knew* she'd dumped you—do you think you hid your wounded puppy-dog look from me? I *pitied* you!"

"You're a bitch."

"Oh, yes, I'm a bitch, and you're on my teat just like you were on hers. Your fucking convictions can't comfort you anymore, but a nice suckle will do just fine."

He stands upright, more upright than before, and looks around. He sniffs and meters out his breath until its normal.

"You're wrong, Chelle."

"I'm wrong? About what?"

"I don't just suckle at any teat. I suckle at ones that have something to offer. You're nothing but a dried up cow."

Her hand blurs in front of him and the sting is immediate across his face and nose. He feels blood pooling in the bridge and he clenches his eyes, using every ounce of body stiffness in his favor, using every inch to not strike back. The blood trickles down his nose and onto his lips.

"*Fuck* you! Talk about dried up! That's what you fucking love—she's a dried up—

"Don't you talk about her! She's more woman than you'll ever be!"

"Oh, really? And how many children has she given you, Dan, huh? How many? I'll bet not as many as me."

"What the fuck are you talking about? You—"

"I didn't get pregnant on a lucky whim just once you know! You stupid asshole! You're so into yourself, you can't even see the signs that are so obvious—"

"Wait!" His eyes burn and his nose throbs, but emotion cracks through his voice. "You're—you're preg—"

"I *was pregnant*." The feral look on her face edges icy scratches down his neck.

His breath ekes in and out, painful, like his chest collapses in on itself. Everything she says slices through him, cold and unmitigated by affection or a lingering sentimentality. Her face is devoid of anything soft. He sees her and he can't stand to look.

"What have you done?" His words are barely audible and for a moment he sees something human in her. But a hard veneer replaces anything shining in her eyes.

"Do you think I'd let you father another child? After your self-righteous beliefs killed our last one?"

He can't swallow, but a sob reaches up to his throat and he almost pitches forward onto her as he falls. She jumps back and he lands on the floor, arms flung over the bed, a dying man draped over a rock in a garden, alone. No sounds, only tears and blood, and he reaches up to feel them, both of them, emitting from his face like a speared martyr.

"No..." His voice crackles through his dry throat, blood drips onto the bedspread, and he stares at it in horror, but can't move to staunch the flow.

Chelle would go into the bathroom and get a towel, to save the bed. She wouldn't want blood on the bed. But she has blood on her hands and his hands are bloody and he opens his mouth in a soundless sob.

He can't hear her, and he only wants her gone, gone and away from him, because he fears her and fears for her.

She has betrayed everything he holds close and he is empty and hollow and he hears himself telling her that she is a murderer.

She can't hear him because she has already gone, but he heard her tell him to leave and never come back to her house, but how could he? How could he possibly return—to this scene? How could he possibly return to so much blood?

∾

How could I have done it?

How could I do it?

Callie's back is against the wall. She hears Ryanne's clear voice singing in the shower and all she can do is press up against the wall of Ryanne's bedroom, pinned by a ghost.

Callie's eyes search the room and the cool air from the air conditioner has her quaking. The numbing effect of the pot has subsided completely, leaving her cold; everything feels even sharper and more acute now.

I couldn't go to the funeral. But if I could have I wouldn't have because you are not dead to me. But I'm dead; an empty body wondering when I will be brave enough to join you.

But I'm afraid, Marin. I'm not like you. I'm afraid you're waiting for me with nothing but anger and vengeance and so I live, I breathe, I walk among the other dead never knowing if I am right or if you're waiting patiently for me, reaching out to me with your hands outstretched, wanting to touch me. But did you ever want to touch me? Was it only in my imagination? Your skin was so soft.

The pills are in your hand and your brown eyes are too wide as you lift the glass in a half-hearted 'cheers'; you drink. I wanted to dash them from your hand because I was so afraid, because I wasn't sure. I didn't know how cold your skin would become or how my missing you literally chars and blackens my insides until the smallest gust of wind blows them away.

I didn't know grief was alive.

I remember your face now like it hovers in front of me and I reach out to touch it and my hand passes through cool air that could be you. You're so close; I strain my eyes and heart, back in time, to bring you here to me. I recapture the feel of your hand in mine and see the tilt of your head as you wait for me to give you your life back with a small handful of pills.

I see the other pills in my hand and I pray that there is enough to let me join you. I kiss your cold lips and will the empty space to absorb what's left of me, too.

I take the pills and swallow them and cover your body with the blue flowered blanket while I cuddle up close to you. I hold you now because I want to hold you forever.

Time moves over me in muted waves, and although the waves are slow, I can't close my eyes. My whole body's been infused with lead, but my eyes are more open than they've ever been. The lead fills my ears so I can't hear them scream. When they pull off the blanket and towels, my interminably open eyes see the blood, and I realize nothing will ever be in color for me again except that.

You are so real to me, still. I remember your phone number and so many times I wanted to call. I wanted to see if death transcends the airwaves like it transcends my memory. But I don't dare call because I feel like I betrayed you. I should have just given you one less. Maybe not the one that made you sleep. Why did you trust me? Didn't you see that the burden was too much? I was never strong like you, Marin. Never. I followed you and you should have told me that the pills were too many. Why did you listen to me? Why can't I buy a whole baggy of the yellow pills, the ones that allow me to go on every day? Why can't I buy them and take them all?

Because I'm a coward and don't know if you're waiting to love me or leave me even more alone than I already am.

I can't fathom tomorrow, I can't even fathom today. I know I can't live and love and marry and birth babies and go on like you never happened. It would be the ultimate betrayal. But it's already started. Only I don't want some husband in my bed, I want you. And instead, she showers in the other room and I betrayed you with her as she washes me and ultimately you, off of her. She fucked us both, and I hope you felt it, too. It was the only thing that has pulled me out of the space in-between. And is that so wrong, Marin? If I'm to be banished here, is it so wrong that I allow some pleasure, some moment of forgetting?

Do I come to you now, as a person who hasn't lived? Or do I come to you later as a person who's hurled herself through this life like a barrel through a window, crashing and breaking everything around me? How many bodies, how many souls, make up for one?

I'm so cold, Marin. I am so afraid. I want to be with you so bad my chest and belly ache and instead, I have her warm body and feel of her hands on me and I've betrayed you so that there's nowhere for me to go. I want you to tell me what to do. I want you to give me a sign to tell me what I should do. I'm brave now. I'm brave. I'll come face you and hear your accusations, hear and bear your anger and disappointment. Or, if I should stay here, tell me where to go; what monastery should I join to devote my entire life to you? The monastery of pleasure? Of pain? The convent of suffering? The abbey of solitude? I can't bear it anymore; I can't turn and not see your face. I want to find you and hold you close, please let me hold you close. I will do anything. I will do anything.

"Who are you talking to?" Ryanne stands in the doorway, arm braced against the door jam.

Callie's eyes open and she surveys the room as if she'd been in a trance. Her eyes are red-rimmed and her lips tremble.

"Callie? Who—what were you doing?"

"I have to go."

"Wait, no you don't—you don't work until six. C'mon, I was going to make us brunch."

"I can't."

"Shit. Look, we've gotta deal with this. You've got to let her go."

Callie shakes her head and hunts the floor for her clothes.

"Callie, it wasn't your fault. *It was an accident!*"

Callie whips around to face her. "And she's gone! I fucked up and she's gone and she shouldn't be gone!" She wipes at her tear-streaked face as she pulls her shirt on without her bra. She searches the floor for her jeans.

"It was an accident! No one needs to know—"

"Someone already knows."

"Who?"

"It doesn't matter, *I* know! You can't just forget someone you loved, someone you killed—"

"You didn't—"

"—whether it was an accident or not doesn't matter, don't you get it? I have to deal with it! I can't let it go—*ever*! I can't let her go!" Callie's voice is ragged as she scoops up the remainder of her things and stumbles toward the front door.

"Callie, wait! I just want you to be okay. I want you to forget—"

"Leave me alone!" Callie slams the front door behind her.

༠༠

He sees Chelle standing in the doorway to his office. She's standing behind Heidi, whose mouth is moving, but Cliff can't hear a word.

Heidi moves to the side as Chelle steps past her and into the office. She stands, waiting expectantly.

"Heidi, that's all. Thanks. Close the door."

Cliff can't take his eyes from her face because her eyes are feral and burning. He moves to stand and she holds out her hand to stop him.

"Don't stand. I just want to know why you bolted last week. What is it about me—"

"It isn't you—"

"Oh my God."

He hangs his head. "I know. But it's true. I don't know why I—I don't know."

Chelle scoots back and sits down demurely in the chair, her delicate movement juxtaposed with her violent glare. "Is it because you're so in love with your wife? She's some—some magical fuck that enraptures men! Is that it?"

He holds out his hands too late to quiet the outburst. "Please. I can't talk here—"

"You can't talk here, you can't fuck there...what *can* you do?"

Cliff's breath heaves out. His teeth grind as his jaw trembles. The desk and his hands merge together in his vision and the smell of her perfume accosts him. He struggles to keep his face blank and scoots his chair back. It's five o'clock.

He stands and smoothes down his pants as he walks to the door.

Chelle doesn't watch him. She stares at the empty space where he'd been sitting as he pokes his head out of his door to excuse his staff and send them home.

The room buzzes with the air conditioner; cold and crisp art line the walls. He waits by the open office door to hear the last, soft goodbye from his assistant and then he walks toward her chair.

"You asked what I can do." Cliff walks behind her and she stays immobile but he hears her breath quicken and sees her shoulders tense.

Good. He wants her to be afraid. He wants her to cower, to lose the power she carries in her hips and eyes and full breasts. Her chest rises and falls and he places his hands on her shoulders for a moment before sliding them down to capture both breasts. She gasps and he squeezes them harder.

Her breathing turns to panting and he clasps his mouth around her neck and bites, drawing a small cry. No more waiting, no more Marilyn, no more timing and cowardice and wondering what someone will say. No more death and secrets and no more thinking. No more. Marilyn's picture hangs on the wall, watching him and the cuckold becomes the performer, wishing her eyes actually blinked from a place near them.

He grabs Chelle's arm and yanks her up, pushing her toward the desk. He shoves her into it and lifts her skirt to find silky cloth separating him from her. Liquid fire spreads through him as he feels his wife's eyes penetrate his every move. The painting he bought for her leans against the wall, commiserating, providing his rhythm.

He glances at Marilyn's photo and digs his fingers into Chelle's hips and ass, sinking his nails in and kneading. The sensation is foreign as he rubs and works her flesh, aware that his hands usually rested on Marilyn's hip bones this way.

He reaches around and finds her damp crotch and can barely hear her moan as he yanks her panties aside and delves into the moisture. She is creamy, slick and Marilyn's eyes follow him as he jerks her silken panties down with a huff of ragged breath.

Chelle raises her ass for him and he unzips and yanks his pants down in time to thrust into her with a cry. The wet sound of him slapping against her is punctuated by sprays of her fluid. His shirt is damp, his pubic hair soaked with it. She groans and opens her legs wider as her juices leak down his thighs and her legs.

The pain is exquisite, the aching in his cock accentuating the burning in his chest; his eyes, rimmed red with unshed tears, remain open as he grips her hair and growls, grunts, fucks, calling out to her to take him and swallow him whole.

Marilyn had always been so tight, and now he realizes it wasn't tight, but unyielding and dry. He almost sneers as he holds the photograph's gaze with fury. He shudders and with one final thrust he groans with a hot burst from himself and a spray of cool fluid from Chelle as she cries out.

They are still. The tears flow onto his cheeks now; they cool and burn all at once.

Their breathing is calibrated, deep and reverent and he traces his hands down her waist, her hips. Placing them on her lower back, he steps away and the reality of his deed is embodied in his slick, rosy cock, the sweltry, musky air around him. Chelle slumps forward, bending her knees as if to rest, but Cliff stands, mesmerized by the thing that had been in her, the thing that makes it all so very real. It's coated in her, covering his hair, his shirt, legs and there is no washing that coating off now.

Marilyn's eyes haven't changed. Marilyn's eyes still twinkle from the wall and from her arms encircling Cliff and for the first time, he sees his image burned next to her, his own eyes looking straight at him. His eyes are hollow, his eyes don't twinkle. They stare at him the way a man stares at his reflection on his forty-something birthday when guests await him as he drinks alone.

He pulls Chelle's skirt down, covering her and can't touch himself to put his cock away. He'd need to wash his hands and he knows there isn't enough water or soap to make them clean.

❧

It's a half-laugh, half-cry as Chelle pulls from the parking lot. She talks to herself to assuage the fluttering inside. Cliff hadn't used a condom.

She'd need to call her doctor and get the Morning After Pill, just in case. Then she'd need to get on regular birth control for the next time.

The next time.

Dan is gone and Cliff could come to her bed. How fitting, to be fucked in the bed where Dan had slept.

She holds her hand up to her mouth as she drives the familiar roads back home. She's afraid to go home alone, now. She isn't sure if Dan will be there after all. He supposedly works until three a.m., but what if he left early and sits in her house, waiting for her? She will have to change the locks first thing in the morning.

The look in Dan's eyes, like he could have ripped her in two.

She swallows heavily and changes lanes suddenly to avoid the right turn into her neighborhood.

Truth is, she's afraid. His face was crazed.

I had every right. It's my body. You are a train-wreck since Marin died. I don't want to bring another baby into this world with a train-wreck for a father.

"I had every right."

She turns up the street onto Sunset Road, the liquor store sign still lit, inviting her. This is where she'd bailed out Callie. This is where she'd seen

Marilyn in the girl's face and body and this is where she felt violated and humiliated, even though the girl doesn't know. She shouldn't know.

And now she's the violator.

She wants the elation to last. Tears pool in her eyes and slide down her cheeks. She pulls into the parking lot of the store and covers her face with her hands.

She jerks her head up and looks around, but all that's there is traffic and a strip mall and a liquor store. She doesn't feel alone anymore, she feels the weight her deed with Cliff like the weight of the dead.

Her mother judges her and she's dead. She hits the steering wheel and curses the roof of her car.

"You were a tired old woman who let herself get beat! It was your fault!"

Her daughter judges her and she's dead. Her chin quakes as her mouth opens in agony.

"And *you*! You could have come to me! *Oh, Marin*! You could have told me—but you told your *fucking father* and you should have known I would have helped you!" Her forehead connects with the steering wheel and her shoulders shudder with her sobs. "Marin, why? *Why!*"

Her unborn child, her father, they all judge her and their clamoring voices surround her and she sobs.

Her mother's voice is alive, it rises above them all, blaming her for fucking Cliff and she wipes at her face, catching her breath.

"No, you don't have a say! None of you has a say..." She sweeps her hair from her face and watched the mascara lines drizzle down her cheeks. Her voice is haggard as she whispers.

"I had every right."

❧

Dave Kleymeier has weatherman hair and Marilyn doesn't like the way it sits on his head like an ice cap. The rest of him is fairly well put together, with well-manicured hands and a shiny wedding band.

But his wife doesn't understand him.

"So, enough about me. I wanted to ask you about your volunteer work. A lot of people would want to put it all behind them. What made you decide to volunteer after your daughter's suicide attempt?"

Marilyn winces. It sounds so simple, and therefore harsh. It loses the nuances that surround it. Callie was young, troubled. Marin had instigated it. Marin had always been the leader.

Marilyn dismisses the question and smiles at him.

"You know, I don't feel like talking about that tonight. It's been a rough day."

His eyes soften. "I think it's been a rough few years. It might do you some good—"

"I've been through all the counseling I need, Dave. Our family worked very hard to get where we are." She can't hold his gaze for long, and his stare is penetrative.

"So you're all just fine n' dandy, huh?"

The reporter must have told him how her little visit with her and Callie had gone. "We have our problems. *Just like everyone else.*" Her stomach twists painfully and she places her hand over it protectively.

"When did you start volunteering for YSPC?"

Marilyn studies his face and the awful thought occurs to her that his motives are actually the story and not her.

"About six months after the incident. Now can't we talk about something else? Pretend we're back on Facebook chat."

He smiles and nods. "Okay, I guess we can do that."

Neither of them speaks; Marilyn sips her club soda gingerly, scrambling to talk about anything but Callie. She misses the anonymity of chat. She can type "brb" and have a moment to gather her thoughts.

She places her hand on the table and moves her middle finger back and forth on the table cloth, watching it, hoping he is as mesmerized by it as she is. When their eyes meet, he's looking at her intently.

"You are... beautiful, Marilyn."

She looks down and up again, eyes twinkling. "Thank you, Dave. That's very sweet."

"And I have a confession."

"A confession?"

"My interest in you goes above and beyond professional, and…I thought you should know that."

He's testing the waters and she enjoys the moment, the familiar feeling of being in control.

"What if I confessed the same thing?"

"Well this is an unexpected and pleasant turn of events, then." His hand covers hers and she lets his thumb caress the top of it. He's more confident now. The warmth of his palm travels up to her neck but her stomach doesn't like it. She pulls her hand away, smiling.

"I have to be careful in public."

"Yeah, me too. So, you and Cliff…?"

The question hangs and she realizes no one has ever asked it before. Her stomach flutters and her hand touches it. "Oh my God."

"What is it?"

She curses herself for the lack of caution. He would know, now, and he does. His eyes travel to her belly and back up to her face.

"You're expecting?"

She sighs with feigned irritation. "The tests say yes."

Dave leans back in his chair, face upturned toward the ceiling. "Je—sus, Marilyn, you're full of surprises, aren't you?"

"I'm sorry, I haven't told anyone—meaning Cliff."

"Are you keeping it?"

She can't keep the mild shock from her face. "Of course!"

"I'm sorry, I didn't mean to offend. It's just, you have a college aged kid, and some people are, you know, done by now."

"Well, I guess I'm not done." She pulls another bit of her bread off of the hunk on her plate and rolls it between her fingers.

"That explains the appetite, or lack thereof, huh?"

"Yes," she laughs, relieved that she could be open about it with someone.

"Let's go celebrate." He chugs his beer and places the bottle back on the white table cloth. "Let's get out of here."

His hand covers hers. Her face reddens and she shifts in her seat. "What do you mean?"

The look in his eyes tells her exactly what he means and her breath quickens. He smiles a crooked smile, not arrogant, not too confident. Just right.

Her thumb slightly moves over his palm and she knows the power this small gesture has. She knows how aware men are of a woman's touch; she knows and uses it whenever she needs to. A touch on the arm, a light hand on the shoulder, a nudge of the elbow or knee. All of that touching culminates into sexual tension, whether the touch is outwardly innocuous or not. But it's never innocuous. She knows, she's always known innately and from early on, the effect a woman's physical body has on them.

The need in his eyes is apparent and Marilyn tells herself the same story she always does, the story of how two people can serve each other's needs without hurting anyone else. It's a story that rarely ends how it starts, but she doesn't ever see the ending played out. That is out of her control. Her domain is merely to take and encompass his heart while he's with her.

Whoever is on the other end can have it back when she's done.

But she can't stand. Exhaustion overtakes her along with a new wave of nausea. The idea that Dan's baby is in her and she would entertain what she was entertaining with Dave is a cold, searing slap on her cheek. What had she been thinking?

"Marilyn?"

"Oh, I'm sorry—what did you say?"

"I asked if you were ready."

She is ready; ready to go out and find Dan and tell him. Ready to finally settle down and do what she could never do with Cliff. The old guilt stings her, now. "Maybe we can still do that interview."

They walk out into the evening and in the parking lot he turns her toward him and kisses her hard on the mouth. She pulls back but he's breathing hard as he leans into her ear. "The fact that your pregnant has had me rock hard since we were inside." He presses his mouth to her neck and, caught off guard, she pushes away from him.

"Wait…"

"I have a place downtown."

Marilyn jumps as she sees a truck pull into the parking lot. Quickly studying it, her eyes discern its color and it isn't Dan, but it's too late. The yearning in her belly starts and she moves away from him.

"Marilyn? You okay?"

"I'm fine."

A young couple exits the truck; it must be prom. The young woman wears a corsage of fresh flowers and baby's breath and her cheeks are shiny like apples. Marilyn swallows heavily and sees herself through an inner window that normally has blinds. Her cheeks are sunken in. Her arms aren't rounded and firm like the girl's, but thin and wiry, and her eyes have age gracing them like a tired, worn drape. The girl's laugh is like bells tinkling and soon Marilyn blinks back tears as she remembers the only safe place she had ever been, and it isn't with Dave and it isn't with Cliff. A place she'd felt young and where her laughter came out like bells.

She wipes at her eyes and sniffs. "I'm—I'm sorry, Dave. I didn't realize it was so late. I can't—I've got to go."

"Look, come sit in my car and we can talk about whatever's bothering you. C'mon."

His hand gently encloses her upper arm and he pulls her toward him. His chest is broad like Dan's, but she guesses it's shaved and smooth and Dan's has hair and the smell of man and his cologne.

"No, I think I have to go."

"I'm not going to let you drive off when you're upset. Just come and sit. Relax. I don't want the last memory of me to be in tears, for God's sake."

She glances up at him and he smiles gently and without thinking she stands on her tip-toes and kisses him on the cheek. Before she can tell him goodbye he grabs her chin and plunges into her mouth; his mouth is hungry and his arms capture her, toppling her slightly off-balance.

She turns her head away after a moment too long, feeling guilty that she has led him this far when she knows she can't lead him any farther.

He kisses her jawbone and whispers in her ear to come with him and he'd help her forget everything and it's so compelling in that way. In the other way it repels her and she hears more laughter like bells ringing through the night and it reminds her that his intentions don't go beyond stripping her and being inside her. She pulls away, eyes searching the dark, her mouth slightly open. Her arms come up and cover her belly, warding his hungry eyes from her. The expression on his face is so confident and all she wants is Dan's face there and a sob nearly escapes her as she sees herself through his eyes, too.

"Goodnight." Her voice cracks, but before she can turn, he grabs her arm again, and she feels the bruise already.

"You're going to seriously walk away? Leave me like this?" He yanks her hand behind her to feel the front of his pants. As she pulls away, his grip tightens. "I thought we were on the same page, Marilyn. You remember Hank? He told me you were a fucking machine. He told me you'd be a great fuck, but you're just a fucking tease, aren't you? A fucking cock tease."

His voice is low and terrifying.

"Let me go. *Now!*" Marilyn wrenches her arm free, and the place on her arm still vibrates with his grip. She strides toward her car and the nape of her neck comes alive with Dave's stare as he continues to speak. She fumbles for her keys, hands quaking. When she slides into the leather seat, she locks the doors and only then can she breathe. She glances at her eyes in the rear view mirror and they are haunted—a spooked hare. Gravel pelts her car as Dave tears out of the parking lot in his SUV. Her eyes watch his profile, stony and enraged and it causes her whole body to stiffen and spasm with fear.

His words reverberate in her head and she keeps thinking of his news story and *My News 4* and how it all fits together, and how it actually doesn't anymore.

The sound of her keys dropping to the floor awakens her and she fumbles for them blindly at her feet. When her cell phone vibrates she cries out and the tears don't stop. There's only one name she wants to see on it and instead, the number is unknown.

7

He knows its dark outside. He can hear the crickets. That, and his eyes had finally stopped straining with the sinking sunlight through the partially open blinds. He'd fallen asleep and he knows it's late. But it doesn't matter. Marilyn isn't home.

Cliff has his arm protectively over his eyes and he's aware that, for all its absurdity, his pants are open and he's exposed.

Before he can reach down to cover himself, his hand jerks back. Moisture still rests under his balls and in his pubic hair. The sensation of spraying fluid hitting his legs shudders through him and his breath deepens while his face forms a grimace. He can't cry. He can't move, he can't call out.

He can't move.

She can't say anything, he reasons. Marilyn has nothing to say to him. He might as well proudly flaunt his white-stained zipper and pants. He imagines her face, staring at him while he tells her what it was like to fuck a real, juicy woman who wanted him. A woman who wanted it from him. Then he'd tell her he knows about Dan. He savors this because Marilyn has always been his and now, he sees that is a lie. She'd admitted to all of them, all but Dan. Dan has a hold over her that no one else has had and that is unacceptable.

We are a family unit.

Dan threatens to destroy that. Cliff must stop it. *Nip it in the bud.* This may be the way to do it.

And then another thought emerges. This was not the arrangement. This is not what he'd said would happen. The one tie that binds Marilyn is the tie Cliff broke. *He never retaliates. He never gets revenge. He would never, ever dare.*

She would leave now. He knows it in his bones as surely as anything he'd ever known before. She had told him once that she would never stay if he fucked someone else.

But she can't say anything to him.

She can't fault him.

He listens to his breathing deepen and tears well up and slide past his temples and into his hair. She won't fault him, but she won't stay.

Cliff has never been good at being alone. He has never been alone, ever since high school when the beautiful Marilyn Beaumont agreed to be his girl and she followed him to college. She followed him to the Midwest, supporting him through podiatry school and then back to Nevada. She had birthed his baby girl and they were a family unit. She had almost left him once, five years ago, but he was there for every chemo treatment, every new setback, diagnosis, every surgery. She needed him then and that was the payoff for all the many times she didn't.

That's the safe place he went when she wasn't home.

He can smell the sex on him and on his hand and the smell threatens to gag him. The smell is no longer heady, but sickening, a reminder of what he had done because Chelle had provoked him.

No.

He'd made the decision long ago with Chelle. He even knew on some level Marilyn might find out. Then she would need him again, fear that he would leave. But that was all just self-delusion. He'd held that belief in front of him to justify hurting her, when really, the only person he'd ever wanted to punish was Chelle's bastard husband. Marilyn's lover.

But not Marilyn. Never her. He'd allowed her to fulfill his selfish fantasies, never wanting to believe they were hers as well. He'd whored out his beautiful wife so that he could get off. He'd whored her out. He'd made her do it and he still makes her do it and a sob reaches his throat and bursts from him as both hands cover his face.

He'd manipulated her so he could have his cake and eat it, too. He so wanted the white picket fence and the baby daughter and the perfect wife and then he sullied her by pushing her to please him in the most rapacious of ways.

He still can't bring himself to touch anything; he pulls his shirt down to cover himself, but his shirt crackles with dried sex. His fingers quake as he fumbles with each button, releasing them agonizingly slow. His eyes remain clenched, as if he can ward off the vision of his sin at the desk. But what he's done is emblazoned in his mind, and the aura of it surrounds him so that he can't imagine ever being free of it.

His shirt falls open and the cold from the air conditioner chills his chest and groin. He shrivels, feels himself retreating into his body and imagines that the frigid air burns his skin, destroys the layer that came in contact with Chelle.

The cold is almost painful and he opens his arms like a supplication, allowing his skin to be cleansed.

All the while he wonders where he can find clothing, how he can hide it, or even if he should try. He's never been good at deception. He carries secrets like an awkward package, unbalanced and incongruous. His eyes tell the tale before his mouth can utter the lie. If Marilyn sees it, would a look of hurt dash across her face? Or worse—indifference?

He opens his arms wider and tilts his head back. Face contorted in pain, he imagines her body under someone else's hands and rather than arousal, his reaction borders on the violent. The vision brings self-loathing that eclipses his act with Chelle. He'd created the monster Marilyn had become. And he'd created the pain she was in.

He is truly the monster. And he knows he has to make it right. He must atone, and he knows how he must do it.

His imminent absolution causes relief to spread across his chest. So much so that he doesn't notice the changing light in front of his eyes, and he doesn't immediately see Marilyn, watching him from the sliver of illumination at his office door.

☙

The three flames move and dance and seem to wax and wane with each heaving breath. He only sees blackness, his forehead resting on his folded forearms. The sea of faces flicker in the lights of the votives as Dan buries his head deep into his arms, hoping to stay invisible while the intonation of the priest carries across the crowd.

"...I believe in the Holy Spirit..."

He doesn't recognize the priest's voice, and he's glad. He wants to be alone, alone in the bustling crowd of all-night vigilants. He has been led here, led to call in sick to work and come to church. He'd packed his things at home in a daze and drove straight here. He has been led here by God and his heart is broken.

"...the resurrection of the body..."

He hears a woman sobbing behind him. He raises his head for a moment, the light of the candles blinding him momentarily. The pain in him bubbles over and his own breathy sobs cause his shoulders to quake.

"...thy kingdom come..."

They all congregate here to pray in Reparation for Sins. The Sins of Abortion. He has been led here. His heart must be filled with love and forgiveness, but it's only filled with pain.

The bustling of the worshipers is punctuated with a hushed silence, and soon he hears Father Britton's familiar voice. He buries his head so that the wooden railing touches his forehead now. Father Britton picks up where the other priest left off, praying for the increase of faith, the increase of hope, the increase of charity. Dan closes his eyes, his head aching from his tears.

When he thinks of his wife, his anger chokes him and he's afraid. He's afraid every person there will call him out and tell him that he brings the spirit of contention and discord to their vigil. Marin's face is only an idea, now, an ephemeral presence with brown eyes and a flash of a smile with teeth so white, and he can't see her face complete anymore. Time has robbed him. His own mind has robbed him.

"...Blessed art Thou among women, and Blessed is the Fruit of Thy Womb, Jesus..."

Soon the meditation begins and only soft sniffles are heard in the chapel. He presses his lips together and wills the anger from his mind. He can only think of the rosary because the thoughts invading his mind are unwanted and violent. And when he thinks of love, he can only see Marilyn's face and this brings a whole other feeling, a complete and utter feeling of despair and shame as he kneels on the floor.

"...Oh Lord, make haste to help me..."

Oh Lord, make haste, please help me.

His third candle flickers and he watches in dismay as it encloses on its own wick and turns into a black stem with a tiny red glow at the tip. Smoke ribbons up and through the air and he can't re-light it without standing from the communion rail.

But he can't let the flame go out. He can't let it stay and smoke and turn into a black, charred thing; no, this flame is alive, *a life*, and only he can reanimate it.

His back spasms slightly as he stands. He casts his gaze down as he approaches the alter candle, a tall, white pillar among an array of flickering flames. He tilts the smaller candle toward the flame, but forgets the melted wax, and soon, the larger candle is snuffed out. He raises his face up just in time to see Father Britton's smiling countenance approaching. He carries a long, tapered candle and without a word, he re-lights the pillar. He waits for Dan to present his votive and he does, tears tracing his cheeks.

He wants to throw his arms around the priest and thank him for helping him, for not allowing his stubborn stupidity to extinguish the light. But he can't, because the priest takes his place again at the alter and begins speaking to the crowd. Dan fancies that the sentiments are only for him.

"...and Thomas, for whom our beloved church is named after, came to the Lord..."

Dan kneels with difficulty, and sets the votive next to the others. Next to Marin, her unborn child, and his unborn child, who is lost to him forever.

A great somnolence threatens him, as if he could curl up in front of the three flames and sleep. He thinks of Our Lord and how He must have felt; His exhaustion, His solitude, and Dan takes in a deep breath, determined to enliven his senses for the entire night. Tonight he stays awake for his dead children. Tonight he prays for their souls and by the end of the night, he will be able to pray for *her* soul, too. He'll be able to forgive her *her* sin.

"…To thee do we cry, poor banished children of Eve; to thee do we send up our sighs, mourning and weeping in this valley of tears…"

A draft from the open door causes the flames to flicker and Dan covers the three flames with his arms and body, protecting them. It's up to him now. It's up to him to save their flickering souls.

"…Glory be to the Father, and to the Son, and to the Holy Spirit…"

Incline Your aid to me, oh God…help me protect them…

"…as it was in the beginning, is now, and ever shall be, world without end…"

My Lord and My God…

"Amen."

∽

Her belly no longer feels like it's a part of her.

Her abdomen is distended and she can't hold it in. Has her child turned on her like everyone else? If Cliff had seen her in the doorway, why hadn't he come to her and wrapped her in his arms?

Because he had been nude and the smell of what he'd done permeated the air like smoke.

He's ashamed and her heart is broken.

Marilyn's tears are blinding her and she hunches over in the car, over the steering wheel as she turns the corner to The Center. One light in the lobby, a beacon. But she can't see it because a gouging pain shoots through her and she screams.

No, no, no, no, no!

She glances up past The Center and the bell tower of St. Rose sits quietly, illuminated and welcoming. She looks around the parking lot and the night crisis worker's car is there. Dan's truck is not. Her eyes squeeze shut at her own thoughts, the unwanted thoughts that he may have returned home to the wife who will never love him or understand him the way she does.

Another pain and Marilyn's body reacts by swerving away from a parking spot; on automatic, she heads toward the ER at St. Rose.

She rehearses her lines for the doctor. She tells him that she thinks she's at least six weeks along. Maybe eight. She scrambles for the date of her last period—her last normal period, and she curses the explosion of pain in her belly because it makes her forget.

She pulls into a parking space in the front and opens the car door. Her legs are numb, and she can't lift them because every movement is laced with agony and with the awareness of her belly, seemingly growing by the moment.

She thinks of the horror movies where the devil plants his seed and the baby comes too quickly. She then realizes no such film exists and she is afraid this is her horror movie and she is the star.

When a young nurse sees her she speaks to her, but Marilyn can't hear her because the pain is deafening. She tries to tell the nurse about the baby, but the baby isn't hers anymore; the baby is Dan's and Cliff's and Dave Kleymeier's and Garn's and Bill's and every other hand and cock that has ever invaded her. She cries out for all of their voices and hands and cocks to leave her and let her have this child in peace.

The wheelchair is moved aside and a stretcher appears. Then, hands are on her and she knows they are there to help, but moving is too much. She cries out and her tears won't stop, and she doesn't know why they all put their hands on her, even though she came to them on her own. Can't they see she's broken? Can't they see she bleeds? Why don't they wrap her in one of their heated blankets and speak soft and soothing words to her and tell her that she is beautiful and safe and loved?

The lights above her whiz by in a long stream of illumination, a row of flickering flames. The staff chants in dissonance, but it's still beautiful. The bells and intercom voices lilt in melodies and she's calm because the baby is coming now, and there's a certain surrender that comes when a baby is ready for life.

The rush of it is supposed to come after, but instead the rush is now. She will tell Dan she loves him with a baby in her arms and he'd see that through all of this pain, she does love him and she'd opened herself up to him at last.

The mask on her face fogs up as she speaks, tries to explain that they must call the father, that he's home with a wife who doesn't understand him. It sounds silly to her, and so she reaches up to remove the mask but the pull of the IV tube in her arm stops her.

They're all speaking to her at once and she can't hear them all. One man speaks to her and his eyes, they seem so compassionate and she wonders if he will be the one who delivers her baby.

But she knows something's gone wrong because everyone moves too fast. The mask comes off and she calls out because it's time.

And then he tells her that what she says isn't true and she screams because in a dream that's the only way they hear. He moves close to her face and she asks if they'll have to open her up, and why can't she deliver as a woman—she did once before and he only shakes his head.

His hands come up as though he leads a liturgy and everyone bows and obeys and she asks him if he's the one who will save her child. And then she hears the words, she hears her name and the word *tumor* and she can't hear anything else because that's not the right name. She tells them to open her up and see, she'd prove it to them but then he brings a light to her eyes and the light is brighter and brighter and as he calls her name she forgets about the baby and forgets about Dan; she forgets about Cliff and all she remembers is when her Callie was born and moments after, when she kissed her downy head with her dry lips and she'd felt blessed.

She knew this would be the same because she saw the blood. Then everything surrounding her was the color of white and light and the weight of her daughter's small body seemed to rest in her arms one last time.

ᔕ

He'd made sure the edges of the wrapping paper lined up perfectly. It's something he'd always done. The roses go around and around and never is there a jarring line to remind the viewer that the rose wrapping paper is just that.

He'd done such a good job that he must use his hand to feel for the edge. Only when he feels it can he see; he'd not matched them up as perfectly as he'd thought. But it doesn't matter now.

Cliff finds the tape and gently pries it from the edge so as to not tear; it's how she would have opened it—with the utmost care. She saved wrapping paper, especially the heavy, thick kind. This paper had gold, shiny gold, on the underside. But he doesn't think of that.

All he can think of now is a phantom child.

She had thought she was pregnant.

She would have told Cliff, if it had been Cliff's child in her mind. She must have somehow known or suspected it wasn't his.

The tape comes off easily and the paper, seemingly relieved to not be bent to his will, flips back away from the painting—Marilyn's gift. He moves the painting off of the stiff blanket of gold, the shiny surface reflecting the muted glow of the window. Finally free, the paper jumps up off of the floor and rolls around itself as if alive, as if it still remembers it had once been bound tight around itself. His heart races at the colors and the anger wells up in him.

Maybe she'd already told the father. Perhaps she'd made the plans to leave already.

He vaguely remembers Dan's face and wonders what he will do when he hears. And he will hear because of Chelle and...*Chelle.* Even through his foggy vision he stirs with her memory. But now the very impetus for her seeing Cliff is gone. Chelle had clearly wanted revenge. Would he be enough for her? And how can he possibly think of her—think of it, *now?*

Cliff lifts the painting up off of the floor and stands, turning around to see where it would fit. Everything is muted and beige and caramel and he stands with this loud splash of color on canvas, defying her, even after she's gone.

He walks to the mantle and leans the painting against the screen. Above it is an impressionistic scene—all in muted colors, of a farm and field. It would have to go. The thought occurs to him to take the painting back, leave the room as she would want it. But the woman in the painting's back is as a lover's to him; he knows every curve, every nuance of color, every line. He couldn't part with her, especially now. Especially now that his flesh and blood lover may have no use for him. Marilyn had robbed him, even in death, of that pleasure.

He rakes his hand through his hair and walks to the center of the room. *What if she had told Dan about her imagined pregnancy?* Some sort of quid pro quo, some sort of maligned tit-for-tat…*My daughter killed your daughter, so I'll give you a child.* The loss they felt so long ago hadn't really touched him like it does now. He remembers the funeral, remembers the mercy of Dan and Chelle as they hugged him and Marilyn, believing that their daughters had had a pact. They were all in it together—sort of. But the Shaws didn't know; they couldn't have known the truth. How could either he or Marilyn have told them? Perhaps Marilyn did the one thing she felt could atone for their daughter's sin. She gave her body to atone. He shakes his head, angry tears burning in his eyes. Where is the atonement for her sins against him?

Cliff shudders and his jaw sets uncomfortably so his teeth grit.

Betrayed; on so many levels, betrayed.

He thinks of her frail form in his office door. When he'd been lying there in his sin, in his shame, nude and unmoving like spooked game. Had she seen him? If she'd seen him, wouldn't she have asked him? Wouldn't she have at least given him a chance to explain? But she didn't. She turned on him, turned her back on him, and left him there alone.

This, together with the phantom pregnancy, gives rise to his indignation. After everything he'd done for her…after everything he'd excused and forgiven.

Guilt stabs at his insides and a dry sob escapes him. How could he be so callous as to cast blame on her now? This must be natural, this anger. He reaches up and plucks the plain painting off of the wall and sets it near the couch. The new piece hangs perfectly in its place. The room feels alive to him and almost void of her presence and this brings a new wave of guilt as he wipes the back of his hand across his cheeks, his breath coming in gasps. It's only a stage of grief, this anger. He knows that he loved Marilyn, and this anger stage is just that: *a stage, a phase, a normal feeling. The stages of grief.*

As he steps back and away from the mantle he hears crackling under his shoe. The rolled wrapping paper remains pristine except for the end, where he's stepping on it. He sits down in the chair and picks up the paper. While still rolled, he tears at the edge and rips a ribbon off. It flurries to the ground in a curly cue. He continues to rip until his feet are bathed in swathes of gold and roses, until he's sure this phase was close to completion.

He is almost sure anger is just a phase.

8

Callie stands at the door, her jaw aching from the way her whole body shakes.

She had not shed a tear and something is so very wrong with her that she hasn't. She sheds more tears for her dead friend than for her mother.

The wait seems endless and finally the door knob stirs. It opens with a rush of cool air and a look of pleasure, then shock, on Dan's face.

"Callie?"

"Hi. Can—can I come in?"

The quaking in her limbs becomes more pronounced and Dan's eyebrows knit in consternation as he moves aside for her and closes the door behind them. "How did you find me—what's wrong?"

"I listened to your voice mail from a while back on my mom's phone. You gave her this address."

Dan stares into her eyes for a long while; finally he looks down, a frown on his face.

"Okay. Well, uh, where's—"

"My mom's gone."

Her voice sounds small, strangled and her throat convulses as she swallows. She wraps her arms around herself and fights to keep composed. She had not planned on the delivery of it to be like this. She had only thought of his face.

Dan looks at her mouth, then her eyes, as if he seeks understanding. He says nothing. He only breathes, shallow and soft. "What do you mean—"

"She died. Early yesterday morning. Or in the night maybe…"

He searches her face, his drained of color. *"How?"*

His breath turns deep and labored now, a look so tortured she can barely stand to watch it. For the first time, she feels unequipped to deal with this task. Fear trickles down the back of her neck and she longs for the heat of the sun on her head. She longs to get away.

Dan's head moves as if hanging by a thread. His face falls in staccato motion toward the carpet.

When he brings his eyes back up, red-rimmed and glassy, she can barely look at him. The icy veneer inside of her corrodes with the deep, fiery blaze of his eyes. She is suddenly unsure of why she felt she should tell him now, this way. She had wanted revenge, wanted to punish him, and now she wants to take it back, take it all back. He moves to speak, and it takes him an excruciatingly long time to form the words. His nose reddens and his mouth trembles and suddenly she sees him as he mourns Marin and then a piece of ice breaks inside of her and she feels a stabbing sensation in her throat. Her voice is choked.

"She was sick. We didn't know."

He nods, as if he'd known, as if he'd understood all along. The silence stretches and Callie clears her throat.

"You left your address on the message—" she repeats, wanting to normalize it.

"Yeah…yeah…I did." He nods and scans the floor, eyes wet with tears. Dan turns and walks to the black leather chair deeper in the room and sits on the edge of the cushion. Callie wonders what would happen if she turned and walked out the front door without saying another word. Instead, she follows him and sits on the couch opposite him. She stares at him, at his face, as he struggles for composure. She wonders why she is so composed. She wonders if it will ever sink in and then she thinks of Marin.

The thought blasts her in the gut, a gaping hole that's empty and cold. She sees the pain in his face and can't imagine what had happened when he'd found out. Her mind races and she fights back the urge to tell him everything, because she can't tell him now; now is not the time. Now he weeps for *her*. Callie's stony resolve returns as she sees the emotion dance on his face for *her*.

Callie wants to scream, tear at his clothes and hair and remind him that he'd lost a daughter. Why should he mourn her mother when he'd lost Marin? The thought that he may have loved her mother singes her and her nails dig into the palms of her hands. She could have dealt with it better if he'd only fucked her mother. That she understood, but not love. Infuriated, Callie's tears surface and when she sniffs them back, Dan's face jerks up to meet her gaze. He seems to come to himself and his eyes clear.

"I'm sorry…Callie, I'm so sorry." His voice cracks. "Jesus, here I am acting like a fucking idiot when you've…can I get you a drink?" He stands and seems eager to be consumed by a task.

"Did you love her?"

She swallows heavily and her mouth is suddenly arid and burning with thirst.

Dan's lips purse he inhales deeply. "We worked together at The Center and we became good friends."

"You didn't answer my question."

His eyes look hollow and lost. His nostrils flare with the effort to speak. "Why did you come?"

"Because from your message on her phone I thought, you know, you'd want to know. Hear about it like this."

His voice cracks and only comes out breathy. "Thank you. For stopping by and telling me."

She stands and grabs her keys out of her pocket. Her hand wipes at her face, her resolve imbuing her words. "My Mom loved my Dad. I'm pretty sure of that much. Oh, I erased it. The message."

Callie opens the front door and she can feel him stand behind her.

"Callie, wait…"

She closes the door, muffling the sound of his voice.

༄

She didn't let him finish; she didn't let him explain. The girl was obviously in pain and wanted something from him, and all he could do was blubber in front of her like an idiot.

Did you love her?

He wracks his brain for the exact words he'd used in his message to her. How many had he left her? How many had she kept? She'd left a message for him recently and hadn't said she'd loved him. He's almost sure. Maybe he responded in kind. Maybe not.

Fuck.

But she knew. The girl knew. Only she wasn't a girl to him. The look in her eyes had been as jaded as the look in his own.

Marilyn.

He had been able to conceive of a world without her just a few short weeks ago when she broke it off with him. He'd never even harbored a hope after that—even after all the recent phone calls and missed connections. He wondered if he had anything of hers that led her to call him lately. A pair of panties. An earring. He wondered which way she wanted to wipe the sidewalk with him. He grabs a bottle of tequila from the bar and pours a shot.

After everything, the one emotion that dogs him now surprises him the most. His face is stony as he stares in the reflective glass at his darkened image. His jaw is set, the muscles protruding. She left him hanging when he had been ready to give everything up for her. He had defied his marriage, his values, even his very core faith and she flicked him off of her like a bug.

He walks to his phone and picks it up, dialing voice mail. He'd saved her last message and he needed to be sure. He pinches the bridge of his nose as the message plays. He drops into his chair and his eyes squeeze shut. He presses 9 to save.

"Dan, hey, it's me. Long time, no talk I guess. Umm…I would like to talk to you, in person, if that's possible. I don't know if it is, but…anyway. Call me. I love you."

ↀ

She had debated on her outfit all night. Last week she'd worn a flowing skirt. Chelle decided a skirt—definitely a skirt again. She'd shaved her legs, shaved her pits, trimmed and perfumed between her legs and slathered her body with sweet-smelling lotion. All in the hopes that the awkward part was over.

When she'd opened the door she knew from Cliff's face the awkward part was only beginning. The news of his wife struck her cold and icy, like a chilling slap across her face. Her hands climb up to the base of her throat and stay there.

She's now sharply aware of the way she smells, the way she looks. She'd dressed for a glass of wine, conversation, hot, intoxicating sex. She wasn't prepared for this. She wonders if Dan knows. She wonders about his face when he finds out. Her fingers dig into her flesh on her arms.

Cliff wants her to say something, do something. She can tell. What can she say that wouldn't come out triumphant? What could she do that wouldn't convey the utter chaos of thoughts running through her mind?

The woman was hurting both of us and she deserves to be dead.

But the moment she thinks it, her insides shrink. She sees the loss in his eyes and she can only imagine the loss that will be in Dan's when he finds out. Even in death, the whore will have them both.

Chelle bows her head, searching for the words that will comfort him, searching for anything genuine.

"I—I'm so sorry. I don't know what to say, it's such a shock."

"Yes. It is—was. I didn't want to tell you over the phone."

"Of course."

Cliff has his hands wedged between his knees, eyes downcast. What does he want from her? She can't possibly offer him the commiseration he needs. She stands and wanders over to the counter in the kitchen.

"Can I get you something to drink, Cliff?"

"Maybe…uh, do you have wine?"

"Is white okay?"

"Yes, thank you."

Chelle pours the pale gold wine, already chilled, into the glasses she'd set out earlier and walks back to the living room. He takes his glass and places it in front of him. She can't imagine he'd shed a tear. He is composed and dignified. Dan would rend his clothes like the infant he is, always over the top, always histrionic.

"How are you holding up?" She wants to be his friend. She wants to forget who he's lost.

Cliff shrugs and gives her a wan smile. "I think I'm still a little numb. Or in shock, or something."

"How's Callie?"

He swallows and his eyes are pained. "She seems…she's alright for the most part. She won't talk to me. She's caught up in friends…school…you know."

Chelle nods and takes a sip of wine. The holidays are coming and the anniversary of Chelle's mother's death approaches. She doesn't think of the other anniversary of death. She can't. The holidays are the worst time—as if there's any time auspicious for death.

"What are you guys doing for Thanksgiving?"

"Oh, I think Callie and I will go out somewhere. They have dinners out, don't they?"

"I'm sure they do."

Cliff stares at his untouched wine glass. His eyes wander to her bare legs and follow them up to her eyes. For one brief moment she sees hunger and she doesn't know how she could make love under such a looming shadow.

"You gonna drink your wine?"

"I—I don't know." The wine lurks in front of them like an emblem; a symbol of her intent. She sees the quandary dance across his face as his eyes return to her bare legs. And how bad would it be to take him to bed after he loses his wife?

Because Marilyn was his wife.

She sips more wine, hoping to numb her mother's voice from her head. But it's her mother's voice and her own, telling her that there are ramifications for fucking with bitterness; fucking for revenge. There are cosmic forces at work and Chelle can see them and her hands are as dirty as anyone's in this. Her evil thoughts, her mindless hatred.

Marilyn was somebody's mother.

But she will now forever be young and beautiful. She will be fair and lovely and remembered in the prime of her life, a constant symbol of love and loss and Chelle will be what is left behind. The left over. She will grow old and wrinkled in front of their eyes, a shadow of luminosity entrenched in a withering form.

She squeezes her eyes shut. When she opens them, she takes in a deep breath, willing to go whatever direction he tells her to go.

"What can I do, Cliff?"

She meets his gaze, unsure of what to do, unsure if she ought to lead him to bed or out the door.

"I'm confused. I—I don't know."

"I don't know either." Inside, she craves his touch, craves his absolution for her evil thoughts. His face is stony and its then she knows.

"I guess maybe I should go," he says.

She searches his face and the lump in her throat keeps her from speaking right away. The way he fingers his keys, ready to bolt; she ought to have known he is only there to say goodbye.

At least he has the decency to do that much.

∽

"But you can't leave. I brought you roses." Callie's manner is distant and oddly playful even though inside, her chest aches painfully. "You can't tell me that."

"I just *did* tell you that. And thanks for the roses." The flowers are still wrapped in plastic, lying on the counter with no water. Ryanne's packing water glasses from her kitchen cupboard. She wraps each one uniformly in a sheet of newspaper. Even the plastic ones.

"Why? Why do you have to go?" Callie sits in front of her on the rickety kitchen chair, balancing her purse on her lap as if she, too, had plans to escape.

"I told you. I got a job doing what I want. And anyway, why do you care? Last we spoke, you told me to, and I quote, *leave you alone.* Unquote."

"I said leave *me* alone. So you didn't quote me right."

Ryanne says nothing, but a momentary glare replaces her indifferent posture.

"The point is," Callie continues, "if you didn't get *that* right, maybe you misunderstood me, ya know, like maybe you didn't hear me right at *all*."

Callie fiddles with the tassels on her handbag. She knows the reasons for holding back, but she doesn't trust herself yet. She doesn't know how it will go over. The other girl might think she's being played, or lied to, even—at first. Until Callie looks into her eyes and proves it.

"I think I heard you just fine, Suburb. Look, it was fun, but I'm looking for more."

"More, like what?"

She looks up from her task, another smudge on her nose from newspaper ink. "Like a person who knows what she wants and knows who she is."

"I know who I am. Ask me. Ask me anything."

Ryanne rolls her eyes and Callie moves the chair back to sit cross-legged on the floor in front of her. "I've gotta talk to you, it's kind of serious. Well, it's way serious, actually."

Ryanne glowers at her. "Right. Because you've been so serious all day."

Callie's nose itches when she lies and it itches and she isn't lying at all. She wonders where the lie hides in her words.

"Okay," she begins softly. "I know this is going to sound...look you can't leave because I have to go to my mom's funeral on Wednesday and I can't go with just my dad."

Ryanne blinks a protracted blink and her chin drops. "That is so monumentally *not* funny and—"

"—I'm not joking—"

"—manipulative I can't even believe it! Me and my hormones! I get all squishy and emotionally involved with some *seriously disturbed train wreck* like you and—what do you mean you aren't joking? It's not funny—"

"No, it *isn't funny*. I know, and I came here to tell you but it seemed a really bad way to start out, but my mom died. And I...don't know what to do." For the first time, she wonders why she can't cry, why she can't conjure anything but an awkward sense of displacement. Her face flushes with blood at the look on Ryanne's face. The look is incredulity.

"Why would you come here and tell me that—like, like *this*!"

"Like what, Ryanne? Like without being all emotional and—"

"Yes! Yes like this, you don't even act like your cat died, and you're... something is *wrong* with you."

"*I know*," she pleads, putting her hand on Ryanne's arm. "I know and I need your help because I don't know what's wrong with me. I should be devastated, right? I should be and all I can...all I am is...numb."

Ryanne's expression softens and she leans closer. "I can't help you *feel*, Callie. I don't know what's wrong with you."

"But I know that you're my friend and if anything, you can help me, ya know, get there—"

"I'm a friend. Great, a friend. And while we're at it, I don't do therapy."

"I don't understand." Callie has a moment when her thoughts turn small, like a pin-prick on paper and all that's left is fear. She sees Ryanne's face and her water glasses in paper and her smudge and her...*gone*, suddenly, and this incites a fear so violent she begins to shake. "I don't understand."

"What did you think would happen here, Callie? Have you stopped to even think about what you plan to do tomorrow, next week? Next year?"

Callie gazes into her eyes. "I never think I'm going to make it that long."

"But you are. You have a life stretching out before you and it's a life without your *own mother* and, incidentally, without me."

Callie's purse topples onto its side and her pill bottle rolls onto the floor slicing into the awful silence. But she doesn't move. She can't. Her mouth is parted with something large, a word and a feeling so big she can't make it come out and so she shakes her head, but the word takes the shape and the form of tears and they roll, big and solid, down her cheeks.

And it isn't Marin she misses, because she went down that road already, and it isn't just her mom, although that thought twists the pain inside her. She sees Ryanne's face move before her and hears the words and the thoughts of not seeing her suddenly collide with the thoughts of her mother never standing in the laundry room to greet her again, and Callie's face crumples and there's nothing she can do now to stop it.

Her mouth remains open and her head tells her to run as fast as she can before Ryanne sees any more of her naked grief, but she's rooted to the spot, pain accentuating every breath, every move she makes. To run now would surely kill her. The stuck word chokes her and she watches Ryanne's forehead crinkle and sees her hands clear away the glasses and papers in front of her as she crawls toward her but the word, the damned word won't come out of her mouth and continues to stream down her face, down her nose.

Ryanne's elbow captures her around the back of her neck and pulls her to her shoulder and only then does sound emanate from her mouth, but still no words. The release takes every muscle, every ounce of flesh on her body because every inch of her quakes and comes alive with each wracking sob.

When Callie takes a breath, more sound comes, and the word, *that word* wriggles its way out of the strangled tube of her throat and out her mouth and it comes out haggard and shrill and Callie screams, *"Sorry!"* And once it comes out of her, she can't for the life of her make it stop.

♋

Memories are misleading at best, deceptive at worst. Sometimes memories get skewed on purpose to defy what's real in the hopes that tomorrow will be a better day, a better world, a world that matches the perfect memory of it. An image can take over a memory, isolating it from the truth. A captured image embodied in a sock stuffed in a drawer, a painting unwrapped or the ringing of an unanswered phone. A sensation of flesh striking flesh.

When loved ones pass on, the memories of them become cemented inside like a monolith. They are larger, they are better, they are bolder than in life. Once filled with strife, a daughter will cling to her mother's voice; a mother to her anger because her daughter didn't listen.

In the mother's lament, they release themselves of the guilt that comes with the loss of a child. The *'what ifs?'* and the *'how comes?'*

The dead have no choice but to betray, and the living, to be angry. It never occurs to the living that their deceased loved ones had little to do with their abandonment. Nurturing the anger is an anesthetic. The living hold onto it, tight against their bosom. In return, anger alleviates the loss and releases those that remain from the horror of having to finally say *goodbye*.

Mourning conjures thoughts of death, but it isn't necessarily so. Every day, the mourning of a hundred minute deaths occurs. The couple who make vows, bright eyed and earnest, couldn't foresee the day when their desire twists resolutely around itself. How could they know that control and lust could become mangled so much so that the young wife takes lovers, one after another, while the husband watches, helpless and inflamed, from the shadows of their bed? He mourns the loss of the day when making love to her came without someone else egging him on, or his own voice whispering to him that he will never be enough.

Innocence is ephemeral and frail, a constant fatality in the daily mechanisms of life. Innocence is mourned when God refuses to protect, and instead condemns and abandons. It is not so easy to forsake beliefs simply because the beliefs damn. Faith is also a common casualty, once resolute and solid, it soon wavers and crumbles into dust.

For all of these losses the one most often mourned is the past. Acts of betrayal, acts not committed; simplicity and naiveté creating a cocoon to inhabit a safe and painless world. A world where conviction equals strength, allure equals invulnerability, and secrets guarantee control.

Kept secrets dull the sharp edges of life. The secrets that eat from the inside out. Nestled inside every soul is the sharpest agony of loving in secret, with no hope of the love ever being returned.

So imaginary and creative recollection ensues. The past is re-created and mourned, but the truth of it remains obfuscated: the past must be laid to rest. Nothing good comes from reanimating the dead.

There is no telling that to Callie, however. She bears the burden of all that desire and death alone. As she looks back, always back, she stumbles upon all that lies before her; like Lot's wife, she turns to salt and is retired to the earth. She doesn't have the courage to follow, nor does she possess the will to carry on. For her, there is nothing after *sorry*.

They were all so very sorry in one way or another. But I know Callie's brand of sorry the best because it was born of a blinding love that eclipsed everything around her. Even now I miss it. I felt it when she touched me, when she looked at me. I even felt it when she killed me.

I hold no blame for her now. I release her. If only she could do the same. But she can't, because she loves me, you see.

ACKNOWLEDGEMENTS

Thanks to the many people who supported me during this endeavor: my superb editor, Shawna Payne-Myers, my Betas, Natalie R. Collins, Aaron Ritchey, Jessica Winward. People who cannot possibly go without acknowledgment for the nature and spirit of this work: Philip Roth, Robert Olen-Butler and Jennifer Egan. Thanks to Dr. Kipton Norris and staff. Your help was invaluable. The best and most profound inspiration and support comes from my husband, E. Thank you for helping me shoot for the stars; thank you for helping me find them in the first place.

~JACW

Follow JA on her website: jacarterwinward.com

www.ingramcontent.com/pod-product-compliance
Lightning Source LLC
Chambersburg PA
CBHW060216180626
46813CB00007B/2842